Thelm

CONTAGION

FOLLY PRESS

Published in 2016 by
The Folly Press
61,Bridle Way
Grantchester
CB3 9NY

For Frank, Ian and Rebecca
In memory of Nicolas
and in tribute to one wonderful Cumbrian village
where these things thankfully did not happen.

Also author, with Hilary Woodward, of *Divorce for Dummies* John Wiley and Sons Ltd 2004.

ISBN: 978-0-9544818-4-1
Printed by BookPrintingUK

Prologue

In the middle of June, 2002, in the crowd at the 233rd Royal Academy's Summer Exhibition in Burlington House, three women stood looking at two large oil paintings.

They were by the same artist and hung together. One was a portrait of an elderly woman; the expression on her face and in her smiling eyes was of understanding, a web of tiny lines intricately traced on her cheeks. The other was a landscape, painted thickly in dark red, purple and orange. It attracted a crowd because viewers recognised its subject matter from newspaper photographs the previous year. It was called "Contagion" and showed an angry conflagration with dark figures moving in its foreground and the hooves of animals sticking out from the flames at violent angles.

The artist was one of the three women. She had strong features set off by long dark hair and was dressed in jeans and a dark pink silken shirt. She had brought the subject of her portrait to see it hung. The older woman's silvery hair was drawn back from her face with a scarf and she was elegantly dressed, sitting on the long leather bench in the middle of the room.

The third woman, who had come with a NADFAS group from Surrey, was in her fifties, thin, modestly dressed, with short, greying hair. She had noticed the artist's name in the catalogue. She shuddered at the fiery landscape and looked long at the portrait. She was about to walk away when she recognised the woman on the bench as the one in the portrait and immediately realised that her companion was the artist. She made as if to speak to her but then changed her mind and walked swiftly away.

Her hurried movement caught the artist's attention and she whispered a name to her companion. Would she go after her? Her friend smiled, as in the portrait, but shook her head.

Chapter One

January 2001

Towards the end of her five hour journey, Polly Creed realised she was driving away from the mountains. After turning off at Penrith, these had been wonderfully sunlit, but now both mountains and sun had disappeared. Had she booked too hastily? Should she have looked more closely at the map? Then, through a tunnel of trees arching over the road, a dome-shaped hump appeared in the distance that gradually became, as she drove towards it, part of a landscape of altogether new mountains. A line of bleak, leaning trees skirted down the fields to her left and behind them ranged a sweep of curving shapes. These must be the Western Fells.

After a left-turn off the main road, the entrance to the village of Milnethwaite was down a long shallow hill. Soon she was passing bungalows and driving into a muddy street between flat stone houses and farm buildings - no numbers, no names, no church, nobody. Then she was out of the village again. She turned the car round in a field gateway and drove irritably back until she saw a young man, cap, torn sweater, trousers tucked into his boots, calling to his dog.

"Excuse me, where is Church Terrace?"

He took off his cap and scratched his head. "Well," he said slowly, teasingly, "I'd say near the church, wouldn't you?"

Polly quelled her impatience. "I'm sorry, but I couldn't even see the church."

He flicked his cap back on. This woman was a stranger all right. Bit of a looker too. Long dark hair and very direct brown-gold eyes. A bit stressed.

"You wouldn't, not from here. You turn down left and you'll see her plain enough. She's a converted barn near the church."

She thanked him curtly and drove off, skidding on the

muddy road. He chuckled to himself. She might be a smart sort of woman but she wasn't used to farm roads.

The church lay below a dip in the road and at its furthest end was a barn with white painted window frames inserted into its long side. There was an opening into a rough yard and a hand-scrawled notice on a bit of wood banged on the gate-post. 'Church Terrace'.

*   *   *

"Met some woman looking for Church Terrace," said Jonty Stewart said to his mother on his way into the kitchen for his tea.

"Church Terrace!" said his father "Why on earth did you call it such a poncy name Ethel. We're not in the Lake District here".

"You've got to keep up with the times," replied his wife of many scheming years. "You said diversify so we're diversifying" and she dished out the potatoes.

"What's she doing coming in the winter, then?"

"She's a painter," said Ethel, "and she's our first winter-let, so you'd better both mind your manners with her."

"Painter is she?" Jonty said. "A bit grumpy if you ask me." He hid his interest in the woman because his mother had always warned him that Milnethwaite had eyes.

"Where's she from then?" Jim asked.

"London," said Ethel with satisfaction. "Some sort of College."

"Well, she won't know what she's letting herself in for here then, will she!"

"I warmed the barn up for her and it's none of our business what she's come for."

They ate the meal in silence until Jonty began his usual argument about the next day's work. He was always trying, without success, to get Jim to change his routines. "When I'm dead, then you can do things your own way," was all he ever got in response.

He only thought of the woman again when he drew his bedroom curtains and saw the light on in the barn. At school he'd been quite good at painting.

*   *   *

"West Cumbria!" a colleague had cried when Polly mentioned where she was going. "I grew up there and you'll either love it or hate it."
Polly had explained that she had always wanted to paint mountains.
"Well you 'll certainly get them, the gloomy things. And rain at the year-end, though, mind you, it rains there all year round."
South East London had become deathly to Polly since November. Every room in the house, the monotony of the shoddy streets, the ink-stained lecture rooms and pre-fabricated college studios, the routines of shopping, cooking, marking, going to bed, the passing comments of her husband, Brian, the unexpected appearances of her grown-up children with their problems, all had aroused an urge to escape.
She and Tom had planned to spend most of her sabbatical together somewhere inspiring for her to paint and somewhere for him near a mainline station. That was before November. Now it was the end of January and she'd come on her own. A converted barn in a hamlet, described as 'off the beaten track' on the West Cumbrian website, was the exact opposite of what they had planned. But she was drawn to its remoteness. She remembered Wordsworth's 'Prelude' from her school days - the sinister shape of Skiddaw in the fading light of dusk looming over the young Wordsworth as he rowed away across the lake. But January was here and she was here and the idea now seemed melodramatic. And it was raining. There was a great hollow in the pit of her stomach as she stopped the car. She remembered her daughter's

last words as she drove away that morning.

"But Mum, it's so far away," Jessica had moaned.

"You'll have your father near," she'd replied briskly "and it's not as if I'm away for long – back for Easter – think of what we can all get done in that time."

*   *   *

After waving her mother off down the road, her car packed with cases, boxes and canvasses, Jessica considered going to bed in her old bedroom, but instead flopped into the big chair in the kitchen. She looked at the freshly tidied surfaces.

"Bit better than usual," she thought. "She ought to go away more often."

Since her year in France, she'd moved to a cheap room round the corner owned by a colleague of her father's. He was letting out two rooms in the house he'd bought for himself after his wife left him. Jessica had taken the ground floor room but had soon come to hate the student upstairs whom she called 'The Oaf.' Her first year flat-mate had decided to quit the course and stay in France and she was lonely without her. If she moved in with her dad for a term, it'd save money and he might be lonely too. Her room in the boring little terrace house was stuffed full of gear she'd never had the energy to unpack. She could do with the space of her old room. She might even get down to some work.

Dad hadn't wanted to be left on his own. She'd heard a row between them over it; well, not a row exactly, but mean comments and long silences. Not living at home any more, she didn't pick up all the vibes. Most of her friends' parents seemed to have separated. She had to listen to their problems all the time – whether they were on their mum's or dad's side, how they hated going back home because it had either been sold or was occupied by their parents' new partners. Her parents were rock solid, she would say somewhat sadly. Considering that her mother was supposed to be this wild artist, she was a fanatic about "family values" and her father was basically a Harris tweed teacher even though he and her mum were lecturing in a College that was said to be trendy.

Heaving herself from the chair, she scooped a few apples out of the fruit bowl and pushed them into her bag along with some chocolate biscuits from the fridge and made for the door. She'd ring Dad this evening to tell him Mum had got off all right. She tapped her grandmother's old barometer in the hall, checked the house key in her pocket and walked up the hill in the winter sunshine.

*   *   *

The sun was shining its last rays on the bay windows and dull brick walls of Fern Road when Brian Creed parked the car. Fern Road ran up a hill at right angles to a main route in and out of the city. The Creed house was at the top with a view across to St Paul's from the landing window. It had not been worth much when they'd bought it but the area had since become gentrified. The doors and window frames of most of the houses were painted slub green or grey and as the winter evening set in, smart lighting could be seen through the windows of long rooms where the inner walls had been knocked through. Their house had not been modernised.

He had left home that morning before Polly's departure, to deal with a student crisis outside London. He was responsible for what used to be called 'teaching practice' but was now called 'Partnership with Schools' and a placement had gone badly wrong. Off and on throughout the day he'd been thinking about Polly's sabbatical, whereas it had never even occurred to him to apply for one.

From the beginning, he'd been her professional senior. He was in his fifth year of teaching when Polly arrived at the school to do teaching practice. They were married as soon as she qualified. When Miles was born, she'd gone back to work after a year and did so even earlier when Jessica was born. He had supported her because they needed both salaries. Later they had both applied, and were both appointed, as lecturers in the same London College. They'd bought 54, Fern Road on the strength of this, just able to afford the mortgage. They were then equally ambitious and enthusiastic. A dynamic duo, they were called.

Then the College had gained university status and Brian moved swiftly up the scale - until he got stuck. He had never fulfilled his early academic promise, probably because he allowed himself to become too useful to the place, whereas Polly had just been appointed to develop a new MA course for Art Teachers. She was seen as 'a bright star,' linking the College with a plethora of modern art galleries and had by then become a skilled as well as a gifted painter. He was proud of what she could do but, truthfully, rather intimidated by her these days. Especially by the absolute determination, disregard almost, with which she had planned this sabbatical. The balance between them had totally shifted over the years. So, what did he really feel about her going off? Honestly, just how much did he begrudge it? He'd never had any time to himself away anywhere. Perhaps he wouldn't know what to do with it if he did, he sighed, whereas Polly always knew exactly what she wanted to do.

And she had left him to deal with Jessica. Their daughter's motivation was worryingly flimsy. Since coming back from France, she'd been moping for some French boyfriend and threatening to give up the course, whereas he and Polly had both been first generation graduates with a mission to succeed. By contrast, Miles, Jessica's elder brother, was an accountant in the city, already earning more than him.

He opened the door into a dark house. He was now going to be alone here for several months.

"Nothing unusual in that," he thought grimly.
'Empty nest syndrome' they called it, though neither of them had stayed in it much. On the contrary, they seemed to have been making sure neither of them ever did. She was always out attending some private viewing or other and he was at his College desk working late. So what would be the difference now? He supposed her total absence brought home the advanced degree of

their separateness and the fact that he minded this far more than she did. And yes, it drove home Polly's greater achievements.

"If you come back with something to show for it," he'd said, "you might be put up to senior lecturer, I suppose. And it would help pay Jess's fees."

"Her debts you mean."

"I don't begrudge you doing it," he'd said.

So why did he? The Faculty Board had readily granted her application despite her high profile job, but that was how it was. What Polly asked for, Polly got.

"Why now?" he'd said, "Jess is so unstable and she needs you."

"We must let Jess learn to make her own decisions," she'd replied. "I think we molly-coddle her. And I've not done anything original for years."

Neither had he, but he didn't say so.

"You don't mind do you?"

He'd said nothing but on the way upstairs to his desk in Miles' old bedroom, he'd murmured,

"It's not like the education department. We just have to keep going."

"Oh, so you do mind," she'd said and he heard her leave the house.

What puzzled him was that she'd chosen a pretty uninspiring spot, as far as he could see from the map. He was thinking that she must have got there by now when the telephone rang. It was not Polly however, but Jessica.

"She got off OK."

"Of course."

"Will you be all right Dad?"

"Of course. I've been looking after myself for a long time. I'm a 'new man' remember."

"I just wondered whether you'd want me back for a few months, you know, just while she's away."

"Good Lord, no. You've got your own life to think of. Don't disrupt yourself on my account. I've got plenty of work to be getting on with."

He put down the telephone more abruptly than he meant. So she thought he'd be lonely. He put on the lights, drew the curtains, switched on the news and was soon asleep. When he woke he recalled that Polly had once said he went to sleep when he didn't know what else to do.

*   *   *

Polly found the key under the stone as Mrs Stewart had described in her letter. She entered straight into a high-ceilinged living room. The windows were all along one side but there was a dormer window on the mezzanine floor where the bed was and where the hayloft would have been. At least that should give a good light for painting. She climbed up to see. There was a fading view of those mountains from the bedroom window. Coming down again, she saw a wood-burning stove with a pile of logs stacked beside it and a fire burning slowly inside. There was a sofa and a good oak Windsor chair in front of a television and an oak table and two chairs at the far end of the room. In the kitchen underneath the bedroom, she found a box of groceries on the counter. The fridge was stocked with milk, butter, ham and some flat, round and floury bread rolls.

"Oh thank you, Mrs Stewart," she said aloud as her dread began to drain away. Perhaps she'd not made such an unwise decision after all. She crossed the cobbled yard to bring in her things. There was no-one about. A brilliant sunset made her stop in her tracks. On impulse she got back in the car and drove off towards it. Fields and villages gave way to an untidy, industrial landscape, but beyond that, from an unlikely place called a 'picnic spot' overlooking the estuary, she stopped. The sunset gloriously reflected in the sea, in a line, stretching towards her from the Scottish hills. She stood there watching and getting cold until the sun went down. It was dark when she arrived back. Really dark. No street lights. After a few false turns off the road, she found the entrance to the yard again, fumbled for the key and spent several minutes finding the lock before opening the door and putting the light on. She would have to get a better light if she was to work in the evenings.

By the time she had eaten and unpacked her things into the sticking drawers of the elderly chest-of-drawers, it was too late to re-light the stove so she filled the hot water bottle left beside the sink and went upstairs to bed. Before falling asleep, she placed a photograph of Brian, Miles, Jessica and herself on the bedside table. Then, as an almost sacramental act, she placed beside it a small pen sketch of Tom. She had drawn it the second time they had been out together – in a restaurant, from across the table, on the back of the menu. She'd found it again, cut it out and framed it, the day of his death.

*   *   *

She was in a car travelling behind Tom's car in the dark going up a hill. She changed gear as she followed him round the left bend. A lorry with blazing headlights was hurtling towards him on the wrong side of the road. Somehow she was between the lorry and Tom's car. Clambering out of her car she was running straight into the lorry's lights waving wildly at the driver to stop. Just as she sprang to one side to avoid the lorry, Tom's car swerved but was hurled hard up against a tree.

She woke suddenly, sat upright and fumbled to put on the light. She was shivering with fear. Was that how it had been? In her dream she had become the woman in the car behind. She thought back to the inquest in a wood-panelled chamber in Salisbury Town Hall where she had seen and heard this woman. The inquest had taken place a month after the accident. She had driven there in the early morning, frozen with grief. She had found the place eventually and had gone inside, praying that she would not be noticed, that no-one would ask who she was or why she was there. The police were on duty. Would they ask who she was before they let her in? They didn't. Would his family ask them to find out who she was? They didn't. There were in fact very few people present, unlike inquests she had seen in films. Just the coroner, the driver of the lorry, the family, the police, herself and the woman.

She had sat in the back row on that December morning, on a hard wooden bench, trying to avoid being conspicuous. She had been shivering with tension much as she was now, sitting up in bed a month later. That dreadful occasion was the last contact with the remnants of Tom's life. The funeral had been bad enough. Several of her colleagues had attended so there was no cause for anyone to wonder about her presence. Brian had seen himself as a close colleague of Tom's because they had regularly met on College committees and had insisted that she come with him "for once". He seemed to think he needed her support. The cruel irony of his request was known only to her. Though she initially refused, she had in fact desperately wanted to be there. She had not prepared herself for the ordeal ahead but she got through the service somehow. As the coffin was borne down the aisle and out of the church, she scrutinised the drawn, tearless face of his widow walking behind it. Did she feel compassion for this woman and for her children, his children? Did she feel guilt? She was so distressed and so determined to conceal her response that she had insisted to Brian that they did not stay to the refreshments afterwards, a fact that Brian assumed to be one more example of her lack of interest in his concerns.

She recalled Tom's widow now in the cold morning as she remembered her at the inquest. She was the exact opposite of Polly. She was grey-haired, slim and a little stooping. Not a confident person, but perhaps grief made people stoop. She had a softness, even a demureness about her, or was it some sort of deference or confusion in the face of the array of prestigious people there? Polly knew that, in comparison, she generally appeared confident and sure of herself. People reacted to her strong features, simple clothes and long hair as if these were statements of style rather than things she had never thought of doing anything much about. People said she looked like a typical artist whereas this woman looked, yes, she looked like a wife, a widow.

In the early hours, she felt anxious again at the risk she had taken in going to both the funeral and the inquest. She was in a panic again as if there were something she hadn't done or something she could have done or could yet do, to prevent what had happened. She repeated the account of his death. She had gone to this macabre inquest to learn what had really happened to him. How had he crashed? Had he been careless? Even, dared she think, had he been thinking about her? They had parted the night before his business trip to the West Country, laughing at how they would manage without the adrenalin of their meetings. They had discussed her sabbatical and how he would contrive to visit her for longish periods away from prying eyes. It was as if by tempting fate they had made it strike.

At the inquest she had recognised his children from the photographs in his wallet - two daughters, both in their teens. One was fair and resembled her mother. The other was dark and had Tom's intelligent, quizzical twist to her mouth. The resemblance took her breath away. She tried to link the girls with what Tom had told her and knew the younger one because she so much took after him. They usually stopped short when talking of their children, complicit in drawing a circle around their affair, not wishing to think where it might lead. On that bleak day his daughters had looked awkward and self-conscious, leaning upon one another at a slight distance from their mother. She knew they would have agonised over what to wear and whether to come. They looked much as Jessica might have looked in the circumstances. The courtroom had become powerfully silent as everyone listened to the evidence of the woman in the car behind. Tom, she said, had taken the bend too fast, in her opinion, and driven into the path of an oncoming lorry. In swerving to avoid it, he had careered out of control into the tree.

"He missed the lorry by a hair's breadth," the woman said.

The lorry driver told the same story and the coroner pronounced a verdict of accidental death. The woman had described how she had stopped, jumped out and been there to see him die. His death seems to have been instant. She had found him slumped upon the wheel and he had given a small last sigh just as she reached him.

"That was all I saw," she said in a quiet voice, "and there was nothing I could do. I had never seen anyone die before."

It occurred to Polly, absurdly, that Tom did not know that he was dead. That made him seem half-alive in some curious way. Someone in the senior common room had said that a sudden death was what he personally wanted and another had remarked that sudden death was harder for those left behind. She bitterly regretted that she had been unable to see him, speak to him, touch him, unable to reconstruct those hours after he left her which led to his death. She was likely to be the last person to see him alive. He would have slept after she left his flat, woken to the alarm and driven his car out of the underground car-park without seeing anyone.

The woman witness went on crying quietly at the end of the hearing. Tom's family did not cry in that room that day. Neither did Polly.

Now she was trying to make sense of both the event and her dream in an out-of-the-way barn in the early morning. She had been suppressing her grief for so long that it was now beginning to leach out. That was what she wanted it to do but pain was constricting her chest and she didn't know how to make it go away. She longed to tell someone about it so that she might cry. Unlike his widow, she had no-one to comfort her or acknowledge her loss.

She had studied his widow at the inquest, for as long as she dared, to see if there were tell-tale signs of their marriage in the way Tom had described it, but could see none. He had assured her that his wife had not known of Polly's existence. She slipped out before the end to avoid seeing her at close quarters lest she should say something to her - the line between silence and blurting out the reason for her presence seemed frighteningly easy to cross, reminding her of the moment when a train careers into a

14

station triggering the crazy thought of jumping in front it.

Shaking herself, she got out of bed, went down the slatted wooden stairs to make some tea and, huddling herself in blankets, lay down on the sofa, staring blankly at the strange room before falling asleep as the dawn broke and the rain began to fall.

*   *   *

The church porch was squat and built of limestone, its interior plastered white like the inside of a cob-nut shell. Polly had taken to sitting there on the rainy days of her first week in order to get an uninterrupted view of the western fells. It reminded her of the cell for an anchoress in the days of Saint Beaga, the local sixth century saint she read about in the church guide-book. She would snatch her pad and crayons and cross the cobbles to the church whenever she saw the fells emerge from cloud and mist. It had rained every day since her arrival, the rain only clearing for a short while. She did not venture far on foot, hesitating to encroach on the life of the village, and it was too wet to explore the fells though she studied them in the maps in the barn.

Her first visit to the nearby small town had been on market day, when the narrow pavements were full and she had to step out into the road. She was hailed from the opposite side of the street by the man she encountered on the day of her arrival.

"Morning Mrs Creed. This'll not help your painting much then."

She had nodded with a half-smile. How did he know her name and what she did? She was glad to escape to her car. Another day, she met the cleaner coming out of the church as she dashed into the porch to escape the rain.

"You'll be the painter lady, I take it," said the woman, in a headscarf, a grey coat pulled together with an ill-matching belt.

"Yes, I am." She was again surprised that she was identified.

"Are you then?" was the non-committal reply.

"And you?" Polly ventured in the ensuing silence.

The woman seemed to ignore the question.

"You'll not find the weather to your liking," she said.

"It's very wet, yes"

"It is that." Another silence fell.

"It seems to rain all the time."

"You'll want it to clear up then."

"Well yes. I can't drive far in this rain to see much so I'm trying to make the most of the porch."

"You would, yes." The woman's abrupt style of conversation was daunting.

"I hope I'm not in anyone's way."

"Not much goes on here in the week."

"Really?"

"Not now we have to share the vicar"

"I see," she said vaguely not understanding at all what was meant.

"I'm just old Alice."

And 'old Alice' walked off up the path. Polly returned to her sketchbook where the fells soon absorbed her concentration. She would draw their outlines with one long undulating pencil line yielding to the next. Using dabs of water-colour in any brief interlude of winter sun, she would try to capture the shadows of the clouds passing quickly over them, revealing one fell one minute and another the next. Colours switched from pink to grey, green to black, their textures fleetingly revealed. They overawed her and she was still content to keep them at a distance.

Deeply engrossed in her work, she became conscious of another presence in the churchyard. A smart elderly woman was leaning on a stick, placing flowers on a large old flat tombstone. She was dressed in an ankle-length, elegant green coat. She wore her silver hair loosely tied back with a matching scarf.

Had she been there while she had talked to 'old Alice'? The woman came across and asked to see what she was doing. Her face, with delicately structured cheekbones, was powdered carefully, her eyes grey, clear and sad. She was quite beautiful. Polly showed her some sketches. The woman named the fells -

Burnbank, Mellbreak, White Fell. She had a soft Cumbrian accent, not as harsh as Alice's or those she had heard in the town.

"Are you from the village?" Polly asked.

"Not any more."

"You once were?"

"I left as a young woman."

As she didn't move off, Polly ventured further.

"Whereabouts did you live in the village?"

"On the moor." She pointed in the direction of the coast.

"Do you come here often?" Both smiled at Polly's obvious remark.

"Since my husband died," and she indicated the grave.

"I'm sorry," Polly said. "That must have been a long marriage."

"We were only together for a few years. And you?"

Polly was caught off guard. Was she asking about her marriage or about her stay? She decided she too would be cautious.

"I'm only here for a couple of months. "

"To paint?"

Polly nodded. "I'm here on my own."

"Good for you," the woman replied surprisingly and turned away. "But I mustn't keep you from your work."

She walked slowly up the path. Her elegance was incongruous in this country churchyard. Polly sighed. She envied ~ her freedom to visit a grave.

Chapter Two

February 2001

On a Monday afternoon, two weeks after Polly's departure, just as Brian was about to go into a Faculty Board meeting, his old friend, Max, now his professor, drew him to one side in the narrow corridor.

'Could we have a word?"

"Certainly."

"Are you free for a drink after this meeting?"

The meeting was turgid and Brian became pre-occupied with a train of thought triggered by Max's request. These board meetings had become much less interesting since Tom Frost's death. Tom's death had shaken him. A good-looking younger man, carefully dressed in fashionable suits in comparison to Brian's easy-going old jackets, he seemed to have everything going for him. He was an innovative thinker, from a fresh discipline that the College needed. He was also a spirited talker and livened up the querulous Faculty meetings where staff pursued their departmental interests at the same time as promoting their own. Tom was no doubt doing the same but managed, as a 'new boy' to make the rest of them feel that pursuing his interests would benefit them too. He would chat affably before and after meetings. His talk of 'feminine models of management' left Brian suspicious but curious. And Tom seemed particularly interested in Brian's views, which made a change from the attitude of the other departmental professors. Since his sudden death, they had not yet decided to replace him as Professor of Business Studies. There was even a suggestion that he would not be replaced. Brian could see that there were moves afoot to divert the funds and students into more mainstream subjects, such as economics. Not education, for sure.

"After all" argued the Professor of Economics, "we'll never compete with the London Business School now."

This would never have been Tom's approach. But, of course, it was in the interests of the Economics bunch who were now getting everything their own way. Brian worried greatly about his own department, sometimes waking up in the early hours with images of notices circulating the College detailing catastrophically falling student numbers and students failing teaching placements which were then lost and irrecoverable. The government's newest policy on the training of teachers had put education departments into turmoil. So much was being devolved to schools under the label of "partnership" that academic rigour was at risk. While he could see logic in paying schools to take students in order to prevent head-teachers from saying they had no spare capacity for training them, this had removed crucial funding from university departments. The bottom line of that was a loss of jobs. And Brian was now in his fifties. Is this what Max wanted to discuss? He struggled through the meeting, aware of the complaining tone of voice he had now come to adopt.

"But Mr Chairman," he would begin, "are we not overlooking…."
and then catch a glimpse of the expressions on the faces of colleagues from the departments currently in the ascendant. 'University politics,' he would sigh afterwards to his administrative assistant whilst wondering how long he would manage to keep her. He used to enjoy his job when education was buoyant and they had more students wanting to come than they had places. He took delight in handling UCCA as it used to be called. He could ask for A and B grades, casually letting it be known that he was turning many applicants away. Not any more! Nowadays he avoided handling admissions. 'I've had my turn' he would say whereas the truth was that he had lost the will to fight.

He and Max pushed through students into the bar of the Anchor and ordered drinks.

"I wanted a word," said Max. "I've been looking up the figures and we have slumped very seriously in the last two years both in numbers and the standards of entry into the department."

"True," replied Brian, "but you must take into account, government policy…."

"No doubt, no doubt at all, but the end result, you know, Brian…"

"There's little more I could do."

"I'm afraid I don't agree," said Max in the clipped tones of a professor.

Recognising his defensive tone before he could correct it, Brian heard himself making excuses. "I've tried everything I could think of…."

"Exactly," said Max, "which is why I am suggesting an overhaul of the whole syllabus and style of teaching."
Brian looked glum.

"You are not looking pleased, Brian." And then, as a non-sequitur, "Is Polly still away?"

"She is." Why was he bringing Polly into this?

"Getting some good work done I trust?"

"I don't know."

"Not visiting her?"
Was he thinking there was something significant about their deal to leave her alone to work?

"She wants to work alone."

"I see."
No, you don't, thought Brian. Was he hinting that he knew something that Brian did not? Perhaps Max was already thinking what the impact would be on Polly if he lost his job or, worse, that Polly had gone because she was bored with him for having lost his drive.

"Well, Brian, not to beat about the bush," continued Max, " I'm asking young Ron McNally to mastermind a review".

"But he's not been here long?" That tone again.

"Precisely the reason, Brian. A fresh approach is what is called for."

"I see." So that was where this was leading.

"I hope you will be helpful to him. After all, you have so much experience"

Which is now expendable, thought Brian. "Of course, Max, of course. Anything I can do," he replied, embarking on his own downfall.

"Good man."

Good man? How did Max come to adopt these clichés with him. They had known each other for years. But, of course, it was to avoid stating what was really in his mind. Letting him down gently. Brian's frustration prompted him to stand up suddenly to go.

"Is that all Max?"

"That's all for the moment Brian. Another drink?"

"No, I have a lot to do". Boring old busy Brian again.

"We must have you and Polly round when she's back."

Polly this and Polly that! "Not until Easter."

"Ah," said Max, managing to imbue the word with inexplicable meaning.

*   *   *

The weather had at last become clear and bright after the first rain-sodden weeks which had mostly confined her to the church porch. Far from coming to a drab area, as she had at first feared, she had come to the most wonderful part of the world, full of contrasts. She was drawing feverishly, in delight over small details - a gateway or a broken down dry stone-wall or a barn window - as well as glorying in the sweeping views of the fells. She discovered Loweswater lake and stopped beside it to watch its changing moods as the shadows of clouds moved across the surface, delighting when the winter sun splintered though the black trees along its edge. She drove through moor-land on her way back home from a round trip and took equal delight in the stark shapes of a row of old mining cottages in the twilight, lining the curve of the moor. She always kept a pen and pencil in her pocket and a store of crayons and different sizes of drawing pads in the glove compartment of her car. She made several sketches of what she saw during the day and brought home a host of ideas for larger paintings.

However, in the long dark evenings, unable to work in the

soft light of the living room, she sat on the sofa, listening to a CD or watching the TV until its poor reception made her switch it off and face the silence again. She began to recollect the events of the past eighteen months, because, she supposed, she was no longer spending all her energy on disguising the impact of Tom's death.

Their first encounter had taken place after a showing of the final year students' art-work in the College's main hall. At this annual event it was a custom for the staff also to exhibit some of their own work for sale. She had two pieces on display – a large abstract and a small water colour of a road leading away beside a house surrounded by trees, with grasses in the foreground. It was very minimal, with small splashes of colour added to black pen lines. She liked its sparseness. It echoed the mood in which she had painted it. To her surprise, when she visited the exhibition she found that it had been sold.

In the staff refectory a few days later, Tom Frost approached her to announce that he had bought the water-colour. She knew from Brian that he had just joined the staff as the new Professor of Business Studies. He asked if he could buy her a coffee.

"I'm Tom Frost."

"Polly Creed."

"I know. I bought your picture. Is it typical of your water colours?"

"I do very few these days."

"Why is that?"

"I'm in the process of changing my style".

"From what to what?"

"From small to large, I suppose, and from water colour to oil, from representation to abstract."

"That sounds pretty familiar."

"It is rather predictable, yes." She felt put down and annoyed.

"That seems dismissive, I'm sorry", he corrected himself. "What I meant to say was that I can relate to the small water colour and its understatement but not yet to the other painting."

"Well, yes, if you bought it, I guess you liked it."

This had not been a good start. She smiled to herself as she remembered her prissiness and suspicion. He had seemed brash, smooth. Now she thought of his openness as refreshing and ached for him. He had been very expressive even at that first meeting whereas Brian often called her cold. She felt cold in bed later that night and fell asleep with the light on.

* * *

The following morning, she sat up in bed and looked out of the window to see the fells clearly, clouds chasing over them. She repeated their names referring to the map she had laid on the bedroom window-sill to identify them. Mellbreak stood out like a craggy cone and seemed to be the focal point from whichever starting place she chose to trace the shapes of the range. On grey days, the contours of the surrounding fells could be depressing, even menacing. But today, they excited her and especially this odd fell.

Later, in the afternoon, she found that if she climbed high enough she could study it, across Loweswater at fairly close range. She made several sketches before the weather began to change and the light fade. In the half-light of her drive home, she decided to begin turning her sketches into a full-sized oil painting. On her return to the barn, she got out her easel, setting it up beside the window where she hoped it would be light enough for daytime work. She then closed the curtains, made supper and sat on the sofa to reflect on what she had seen. But soon, more memories of Tom came to the surface and she began to re-enact a conversation.

"Look here," Tom had said, picking up her cautious mood at the end of that first encounter, "This is not going well. I feel very ignorant about painting but I felt moved by this one. I just wanted to say so."

"Thank you." She got up to go.

"Please don't go yet."

She sat down again, out of politeness.

"I want to learn more. How do I do this?"

"Well, just go and look at things, I suppose."

"Will you show me?"

She was startled, put off, by such an approach. But he was a new professor and she was a senior member of staff. She couldn't just dismiss him out of hand.

"That's an unusual request."

"I think you are an unusual person."

That had sounded like a come-on. "You don't know me," she'd said in a stilted way.

"I should like to get to know you."

"Do you always approach colleagues in this way?" She spoke like a school-mistress.

He laughed. "No, but I've always worked with colleagues in the same line. Here there are so many different skills and I want to learn. I thought, having bought your picture…"

"…you could buy me?"

"Well, I am a business man!" he laughed again. " I'm afraid it shows."

"I'm afraid it does," relaxing a little at his transparency. Now she recalled his teasing with a smile as she sat looking into the stove.

"Think it over," he'd said and offered his hand as he rose to go. She took it and it was warm and inviting.

She did think of him again because she spent the next few days trying to avoid him. Eventually, he hailed her across the refectory.

"Can I join you?"

She was with colleagues and had no option but to introduce him. He chatted amiably with them until she rose to go when he also rose and followed her.

"I'm sorry I was so crass the other day."

She shrugged, opening out her hands in a way that, as she repeated it, sitting on the barn's sofa, seemed visibly self-conscious. Not characteristic of her at all, but it showed her now that her acute physical awareness of him had begun instantly and unconsciously.

"I do really want to get to know you."

"I am not used to this approach."

He'd often mimicked this comment later in their love-making. "OK! So you're not used to this approach!"

"All right," he had said "I am very attracted to you as well as your paintings and want to get to know you. Can I see more of your work? Where do you keep it?"

This was like asking to see her etchings! She smiled in recollection.

"Some at the studio, some at home."

"You are married aren't you?" he said abruptly.

"Yes. Are you?" She had said this with a direct eye-to-eye challenge.

"Yes."

She had shrugged as if to say that must be the end of that, take care, whereas he had not faltered nor taken his eyes from hers.

*   *   *

On Tuesdays, the country bus stopped at Milnethwaite. Several women got out, shouting cheerfully to each other as they did every Tuesday. Although Ethel might drive the car into town other days, she chose to go by bus on Tuesdays, to do her bit to ensure that the bus company kept it running for those without cars – like Alice. It was a good day for shopping as the town was not as busy as on market day.

"I've met that painter lady of yours," said Alice, as she and Ethel stepped down onto the road. Alice always hoped that Ethel would speak to her. It picked her out nicely as Ethel was an important person in the village.

"You would, yes." Ethel replied. "

"Doing you all a bit of good, I'll be bound." Alice liked to appear worldly about money, having little of it, thought Ethel.

"It is that," said Ethel." It's all diversifying you know."

"So that's what they call it do they? " said Alice not

understanding."She's a good-looking woman, I'll say that for her."

"She's a very *nice* woman," said Ethel decisively. From the start she would put a stop to any adverse comment from Alice about her new tenant who would, she hoped, be the first of many; it was Alice who could spread suspicion about 'strangers.'

"Is she then? And what sort of pictures does she paint?" said Alice.

"Jonty reckons she'll be painting in oils."

"Does he then?" said Alice with a knowing look and an upward clench of her chin to suggest that she, old Alice, knew a thing or two. "He's been watching her, has he?"

"No. But he used to fancy himself as a painter when he was a boy," said Ethel, regretting her slip.

"I'll have to have to ask her myself then," said Alice "or ask him," as the two women parted company at the lane-end.

"Look after yourself Alice."

"I will."

Ethel guessed that Alice would now be working on what she had foolishly said to her. Of course her son worried her. He was well over thirty. But she did not want old Alice spreading rumours every time a woman came to stay in the village. This first one was, after all, a middle-aged lady though she was not sure whether she was married or not as she had only signed herself. 'Polly Creed'. And she must be a lot older than Jonty. Although she didn't look it, she must be forty-five at least!

*   *   *

After a day working on her Mellbreak canvas, Polly reconstructed how exactly Tom had pursued her. He had told her that he had been watching her from his first day in the place, finding himself one day in the salad queue, caught off guard by her 'hair and vivacity'. When he found her name and then her painting, he sought her out. The fluid black lines and the flashes of colour in her picture reminded him, he said, of the thrill of glimpsing a kingfisher, yet the bleakness of the picture also filled him with longing. On her guard still, she could not have remained uninterested in what this revealed about himself.

He said he had been in a volatile state of mind ever since he'd moved from the world of business to 'this exciting college.' He was head-hunted to set up a department. With a Ph.D in economics he had made money in the city and had become a pundit on business affairs, often commenting on BBC news programmes. She visualised him as she had eventually seen him on Newsnight. Brian had been excited and had called to her to watch. Relaxed, animated, greying hair cut close to his head, and that wry look about his mouth and his form of humour glinting in his eyes. And wearing a beautifully tailored jacket!

As she left his London flat the frantic day there after he died, she had fingered his suits and jackets still hanging tidily in the wardrobe. What had happened to them, she now wondered? Had they gone to Oxfam? She shuddered. All she had retained of his clothes was a monographed handkerchief which she had brought with her at the last moment of packing so that Brian would never find it. Such was the level of secrecy to which she had become accustomed.

Tom had later explained that setting up a new university department with no experience of higher education gave him a kick. He relished designing his own course, attracting like-minded colleagues and setting up research projects here and abroad. The invitation came at a time of inner restlessness. This was the point when he had confided that his marriage had become conventional and sexless.

"In fact," he had laughed, "I am a prime candidate for a mid-life crisis."

The emotional directness of this admission sparked off a totally unexpected sexual charge in her. "Infatuated" was the word she would have used to describe her subsequent behaviour if she had observed it in others. The word usually meant being driven blindly and unwisely - and she was - and their affair began. From the start they took careful measures to ensure that no-one should see them together. They stopped meeting at the College altogether and the colleagues who had initially teased her on his account, soon lost interest. Brian knew him as a colleague on committees and would speak appreciatively of his contribution as a 'breath of fresh air', 'a sound business head', someone who 'cut the crap'. He wanted to invite him to dinner, but Polly said she was too busy which Brian probably added to his evidence of her lack of interest in anything but her own work. She was sure he also saw it as a lack of interest in him. Now, far away in Cumbria, she was astonished that no-one had discovered the affair in over a year. And then November happened. No-one had known of it and so now no-one need ever know.

That night in bed, high in the barn, she again woke in terror. Had she failed to check everything in the flat? What did he have with him of hers in the car? Had he left clues on his body that could lead his wife to suspect someone, perhaps even Polly? She reached out in the dark for his handkerchief in the drawer of the bedside cupboard. What did he have of hers apart from the painting? They never had photos of each other. How did he note their meetings in his diary. The diary could have been handed to his wife by the police. She had discovered that she had lost an ear-ring when she had sorted them out before leaving London. Was that in the flat? Could it be under the bed? In her hasty visit to check that dreadful day, she had not looked under the bed!

She got up, put the light on and paced about the bedroom. It was two o'clock in the morning. Eventually she went downstairs, warmed her hot water bottle and sat hugging it, hands round a cup of tea. She retraced the day of his death. She had learnt of it in the common room in the evening. The Vice-Chancellor had come in to tell whoever was there and to post a notice on the board. Strangely, it was Brian who was there. He had run to her studio to tell her and from there to the common room to look for her. She had faced a gargantuan challenge – to absorb its impact without showing an excessive reaction to a colleague's sudden death. She was by then so schooled in deception that she had done this successfully and it was made easier because it was Brian who thought himself the more upset of the two. He talked of Tom's value and the confidence he scattered around him.

"It could happen to any one of us," he kept saying.

She had stayed in the studio in a state of shock after Brian had gone back to his office. The following morning, after a totally sleepless night, she had driven off at nine o'clock to Tom's flat. As soon as she put the key in the door and stepped inside, she had begun to sob, breaking into dreadful howls of grief that seemed to come from some primeval part of herself. Just as she had been physically in thrall to him, so she was being physically torn from him. She had eventually stifled her sobs in order to search the flat to remove any signs of their relationship. She was afraid that his wife would have the same impulse to visit, even perhaps, on the same day.

Now she was fearing that she had not searched everywhere. In her early morning alarm, she went over every bit of the flat in her imagination wondering if she had removed her spare mackintosh and her spare umbrella. Had she checked the bathroom cabinet thoroughly? What about the sheets? She had pulled them off the bed fearing a tell-tale smell and pushed them into the laundry basket. Tom might well have left them to be laundered, she reasoned at the time, but what sense would his wife have made of the fact that they were there. Did they smell of her as well as of him? She paced about the room reliving her terrors, not daring to return to her bed in case she were to be awoken by more.

When she awoke on the sofa, it was past her usual breakfast-time. Her mind must have been working during sleep because she now recalled an event that had taken place shortly before Tom had died. Would Miles, her son, mention to Brian how they had once seen each other in town one evening?

She had seen Miles coming out of a restaurant as she and Tom were entering another on the opposite side of the street in Soho. In an instant she had read the nature of her son's relationship with the young woman with him. She also knew for certain that he had seen her and that he knew she had seen him.

His companion was attractive, perhaps older than him, with the long blond hair of so many young women, self-assured and laughing. Not like his previous girlfriends, she had thought. The way he held the door open for her and touched her arm made Polly sure that he was in love. Could he equally well have read the nature of her relationship with Tom? As if by prior agreement, he did not acknowledge her nor she him. Mother and son had entered a strange, unspoken collusion. They had never spoken of it since.

For that to occur to her now, told her that fear of the discovery of the affair had become such a feature of her life that it was still poking fingers into her grief. On one level, the risk of exposure was that it would damage Tom's reputation as well as her own and Brian's, as their marriage had become an icon of faithfulness in a senior common room better known for infidelity. Below this lay her reluctance, resistance, to confront the effect on the marriage itself. That still lurked like a dragon at the bottom of one of these lakes.

*   *   *

Early the following morning, Jonty heard his father moving about. It was five thirty. He had taken to leaving his curtains open since the painter lady had moved in. He liked to think that there was this woman asleep in the barn where he'd played as a child - all poshed up now with smart paint and smart curtains and a new soft bed . He went to the window and, sure enough, as yesterday, her light was on. What was she doing awake at this time of the morning? It wasn't as if the birds had started singing? He'd keep an eye out for her and maybe make a joke of it.

*   *   *

Later that morning, in the church porch, Polly saw Alice

again, walking with her dog to the church. She had put up her easel in the porch to map out a view of the fells. After tying up the dog to the boot scraper, Alice made as if to push past Polly to get in to clean the church.

"You working in here again then?" she said.

"I am, yes, Alice."

"You remember my name then." Alice smiled in a knowing way.

"I do indeed. And mine is Polly."

"You're doing the fells?"

"I'm trying."

"You're finding them hard ?" Alice managed to convey satisfaction that her fells were a challenge to a woman from London.

"Well, to capture the shapes, yes."

Alice looked at the canvas for a long time, puzzled. "And have you captured 'em, d' you think?" she said.

"Do you think so?"

"Is that them fells over there?"

"It is."

"Well, I never." Impressionism ands Abstraction was clearly beyond Alice's experience, as was tact, chuckled Polly to herself.

Alice made more wondering sounds in Polly's ear. "Did you know that young Jonty used to paint a bit?"

"Jonty?"

"Ethel's son?"

"Oh, you mean Mrs Stewart, her son."

"That's him".

"I didn't know, no."

"Didn't you then?" creating the impression that she knew what others didn't.

"What does he paint in?"

"In?" said Alice uncertainly. Did she mean overalls?

"I mean, oils or water colour?"

"Oh. I dunno. He used to put them in the village show

though."

"I must talk to him about it some time."

"You could. Aye."

"I think I know who you mean."

"He's the only young man left around here unmarried," said Alice. "You can't miss him."

After she had gone, Polly wondered what that had been about. Looking at her canvas, she realised that it wasn't exactly Heaton Cooper. The vastness she was trying to capture did look more like a Francis Bacon carcass. She chuckled to herself. She had started with distant shapes seen through the rain. When the weather had cleared, she would try a bolder approach, recalling that conversation with Tom.

*   *   *

Polly made a trip into town on the next Auction day. After a week of poor nights she had decided to look in the auction rooms for a directional lamp. The town was full; it was market day for animals as well as the auction of household objects she had seen advertised in the freebie put through her door.

The auction took place in a building across the road from the cattle market. It was a large round space, with the auctioneer's desk faced by an arc of tiered wooden benches. The goods were laid out on a table in the front or an assistant brought them in one by one. Just before the sale had begun, Polly had found a lamp she wanted and several old picture frames propped against the perimeter wall. However, she became fascinated by the sale of china, cutlery, linen, bedding and junk, realising that people were buying the contents of an elderly person's life whom they knew. Instead of bidding as others were doing, she began to sketch the objects and people around her. Then her eye was caught by a wonderfully bright pegged rug. Its colours and textures were rich and varied and she bid for it, aware of all eyes upon her. The price of the rug went up and up but she eventually acquired it. She turned to her neighbour.

"What do I do now?"

"You give the girl your name and the money and collect it after the sale is over. Go on, love, over there."

As the only bidder, she acquired the lamp and three dark pictures that she bought for the frames.

By the end of the morning she had an awkwardly shaped lamp, three large frames and a bulky rug to get to the car-park some distance away. At that point she was hailed by the young man she now knew to be Jonty.

"Want a hand?"

"Oh yes, please."

"Buying rugs? Has me Mum not given you enough on the floor?"

"Oh no. Nothing like that. I just thought it was beautiful."

"It looks like the ones my grandma makes. Old fashioned things. She shows them at the Loweswater Show."

"I'm not surprised. They're lovely."

"Interested in old crafts are you then?"

"Well, I could be and the lamp is to give me more light to paint by."

"And you like these paintings then?"

"No, no. I am always looking for frames."

He carried the lot with ease down the High Street.

"I used to paint a bit," he said.

"So Alice told me."

"She did, did she? She's a nosy old body. You want to watch her."

"Thanks for the warning."

As they neared the car he ventured his prepared quip. "You wake early in the morning don't you? Can't you sleep?"

"Sometimes I wake early, yes."

"You're not cold are you? I'll ask me Mum for more bedding if you like."

"No, no, please don't."

He helped her load the stuff in the car. "Can I see some of your paintings some time?"

"Well, I have little to show yet."

"Mebbe you'd look at some of mine."

"Of course."

"I'll call then."

She watched with foreboding as he walked off whistling. She very much wanted to keep to herself.

*   *   *

Jessica was miserable and there was no telephone in the place where her crazy mother was living. She had to leave a message at some farm or other or try her mobile which was never switched on. Apart from saying she'd arrived, there had been no word from her. They were very different, her mother dark and gorgeous, she sandy-haired and freckled and, her mother said, as gritty and irritable as sand. But her mother did at least try to understand her whereas her moods frightened her father who had no idea how to deal with them other than to disappear and wait until they were over. She thought that was why he didn't want her to move back home. Her mother was more of a free spirit but she supposed she had her father's moroseness. He must have thought that, left together, they would sink into some sort of bog.

Jessica was miserable on her own account at present. She didn't want to work and she didn't want to go her friend's wedding this coming Easter because she had no boyfriend to take and wondered whether she ever would have. She had met Pierre in France and thought of going back over there instead. She was also missing her grandmother who always saw her point of view. In fact she was feeling so miserable she was probably not very well.

*   *   *

The day after the auction, it was raining again and Polly returned to the church porch. She arrived at the same time as the silver-haired woman. They both smiled.

"Perhaps we should introduce ourselves. I'm Veronica Cornfrew."

"And I'm Polly Creed and I am staying in Church Terrace."

"Church Terrace?"

"Oh, it's the barn at the back of the church."

"Ah, the Stewart's old barn. I'm very pleased to meet you again, Polly."

"And I you," replied Polly truthfully.

"We seem to be meeting again in the rain," said Veronica "but that is not unusual here as you will have found out by now."

"I certainly have."

"I hope it's not curtailing your painting too much?"

"Well, it means that I haven't been able to get on as quickly as I'd hoped, so I'm just trying out lines and colours today."

"Do you normally paint in oils?"

"Increasingly so, yes." Polly sat down on the chair she'd brought with her.

"And do you often paint mountains?"

"Never before but now they interest me." Polly assembled her crayons.

"Because they are beautiful or for other reasons?"

"They hide a world behind them, I suppose."

"Ah," replied Veronica. "I think I know what you mean."

"You do?"

"We are a bit like mountains in that respect."

Polly stopped painting. "How exactly?" she asked.

"I told you that I'd only been married a fairly short time but I had actually known my husband a long, long time."

"I see."

My husband was only free to marry me when his wife died."

"Uneasily aware of the unexpected intimacy of the conversation, Polly kept her eyes on her work.

"I left the village as a young woman", the older woman

continued, "and then stayed away and now I keep coming back - but only to his grave. Strange how things work out."

"Indeed."

"I suppose I am telling you this as you may hear of it from others before long."

"I talk to no-one here, except for someone called Alice."

"Yes. I have seen her talking to you. Alice would tell you the story soon enough. Well, her view of it, I should say."

"I should take care with her then?"

"If you have a story, guard it well," she laughed.

She turned and walked away up the path. After a few steps she paused, "I'd very much like to see some of your paintings, if you'd allow me to."

Chapter Three

One morning in February, three months to the day since her husband was killed, Marjorie Frost woke as usual to the sound of the milkman. But today was not to be usual. She drew the heavy brocade curtains and looked out onto the white misty garden. Today she would begin the construction of her new life. This was to centre around her children and her parents. She must live as if Tom had never existed. She would not stay in this house a moment longer than necessary.

Laura and Kathryn had been attending a boarding school in Yorkshire against her will. Once Tom had begun to earn 'serious money' he had insisted on their private education. Now she could turn defeat into victory by selling up and moving north.

"I am not in favour, Tom" she had said at the time, voicing her life-long objection to private education.

"But we can afford it."

"It is socially divisive."

"Utter Rot."

"Neither of us went to private schools."

"We can give them the start we never had."

She saw his face tighten round the mouth and eyes as it always did when he was challenged.

"I insist," was his final comment and she knew she would yield as she always did.

"Only if it's near my parents." This one condition was her only small hold on power.

"Deal," he had replied, so that, she knew he would not have to think of himself as having bullied her.

From then on, while Tom built up his career in the city, she had been left to nurture her daughters from a distance. She did this by staying at intervals in term-time with her parents where she felt rooted. Her parents' home was small and unpretentious, its blackened, square stones in stark contrast to the mock Tudor and red-tiled roof of this Surrey house. The garden was long and thin and open to the neighbours, not wide and ranging and hidden behind suburban trees as was this. It was suffused with clouds of soft, sweet-smelling cottage flowers that her father grew lovingly from seed, scattering them in clumps without a grand design, not sculpted with ceremonial, herbaceous borders, laid out by the paid gardener. She was as certain of its every corner and of herself within it as she was uncertain in her marital home. At her sourest moments, she thought that her life with Tom had been all pretence. She had been happy neither with suburban life nor with the wealth to sustain it, especially as she had no idea how it had been earned, of what it consisted and now, where it was to be found.

She and Tom had met at university where straight from school, she had modestly studied history. Tom was an economist whose lack of modesty had then appealed to her. They had stayed in the same city after graduation and there she just about kept pace with him. It was the move to the London finance company and to their Surrey home that began their slow estrangement. He commuted to his firm in the city, progressing to work with 'stocks and shares' when she saw him less and less. He became prominent in the media for reasons that she did not understand and she soon lost track of where he was and what he was doing at the same time as seeing him frequently on her television screen. Of late, she would switch the set off immediately whereas once she would have called her daughters to watch him. His telephone calls became routes to conversations with them and when they went away to school, they virtually ceased. Tom would take the girls abroad for holidays while she went to care for her parents. On occasional weekends at home, he played golf and bridge and they entertained and were entertained. A few friends may have guessed that all was not as it seemed but Tom was such good company, especially since he appeared on television, that people were eager to invite him. No-one would detect anything unusual from his frequent absences anyway because in their social circle absent husbands were the norm. She occupied herself with helping in a charity shop and belonging to a local Arts Society.

And that was her life until the day he was killed. Typically she had not been the first to be told; because his car was owned and registered by his previous firm, it was they who were first given the news. When she was eventually visited by a police officer, it was her daughters' welfare that dominated her response. She drove to York immediately to bring them home. From then onwards she attempted to organise the funeral together with Tom's solicitor who seemed to know better than she, what kind of event was necessary. Most of the people at his funeral were totally unknown to her. To her incredulity the funeral addresses by the Principal of the College and the Chairman of his city firm spoke admiringly of his personal warmth as well as his meteoric career. How had it all gone so wrong with her? The girls were shattered of course, uncertain how to behave and discomforted by all the strangers around them. She was numb. At her insistence, the cremation, at least, was private. In the last resort, the three of them and the funeral director cremated the man she thought she knew.

Then she had begun to piece his life together. Letters came from all directions from unknown people. She had known he had a flat in London but not the address. She had known he stayed for periods in the USA but not that he had a flat in New York. She knew that he was well known in Brussels but not that he had a regular booking at a hotel there. His solicitor and his multifarious colleagues seemed to know infinitely more about him than she did, but clearly none of them knew the whole. In his will, unknown to her, he had left their daughters protected by a trust. For her, there was the house. The ownership of the flats in London, apparently, and in New York were 'not yet clarified' and whatever was left in his many accounts 'was being calculated'. And as for his private life, since she had ceased to share it, she could only imagine it. She took it for granted that there were other women. After learning of one or two in the early years, she had become studiously incurious, only angry on her daughters' behalf for the pretence that she was expected to maintain. So when she found an ear-ring on her one and only visit to his stylish London flat two days after his death, she pocketed it with a complicated sense of justice.

$*$ $*$ $*$

In her fourth week away, Polly was awoken by the sun streaming through the downstairs windows. From her west-facing bedroom, the fells were clear and the sky was blue with big white clouds. She had worked out where she would go when such a morning arrived . She would drive to Loweswater at the foot of Mellbreak and look up at 'her' mountain.

She parked in the gateway of a field beside the lake. She carried her lunch, a collapsible stool, her easel, an A 4 pad of rough water-colour paper, pencils, and water-colours. She climbed a gate and walked slowly up a sloping field, past munching sheep, bleating and lurching clumsily away when she came too close. She made her way through soft grass beside a dry stone wall that skirted the end of the lake, climbing a stile and avoiding the mud that was the remnant of the past sodden weeks. She set up her easel facing the fell across the full length of the lake.

The water was shining and astonishingly blue. To her right was Holme Wood, some trees dark and evergreen, some bare and wintry, stepping in lines down Burnbank Fell to the lakeside. In the curve of the lake was a farmhouse, which together with the barns beside it caught the light and shade like a trick picture of a pile of cubes that can be looked at one way or another. To her left, tiny streams made runnels between the high crevices of White Fell, spattered with snow. And ahead, Mellbreak's sharp contours stood out, about to become as familiar to her as the lines on the moon to astronomers.

She sat down, awed by the huge masses around her and the privileged privacy they afforded her. This was just what she had sought. Was she capable of responding? How would she translate this detail, clear on a sunny February morning, to the bold statement of colour and shape she aimed for? She must not rush. She first began to draw like a school-girl, trying faithfully to copy every detail. Subsequent drawings omitted more and more detail. Finally, as her lines became heavier and heavier the vast craggy fell began to take on its unique and formidable character. Then she began to apply pools of water-colour to guide her later when she got back to her oils and canvas.

She had arrived at about ten o'clock and apart from coffee and a sandwich, she gazed and drew and painted all day, ignoring the cold in her feet and fingers. Her eyes did not turn away until the sun went down and the lake became inky and the fells dark blue. She made her way back to the car as darkness was gathering. She knew she would sleep peacefully for the first time since her arrival. Brian used to say that children needed to be allowed to complete an experience and she had completed an experience that day.

*   *   *

When she got back to the barn she found a note pushed under the door. It was from Ethel Stewart telling her that her daughter had telephoned and offering her the use of the farm telephone to ring back in case anything was wrong. She tried to phone from her mobile but there was no signal so she walked through the dark village street to the farmhouse kitchen door. It was opened by the young man who drove her back from the auction.

"Come on in, Missus."

"I had a note from your mother."

"She's at the W.I."

"My daughter phoned and asked me to phone back. Unfortunately I can't get a signal on my mobile."

"No, you wouldn't. Not here. It's the fells."

"Your mother said I could use your phone."

"Come through the kitchen if you don't mind my mucky clothes. I've been cleaning off my boots. You'd best use the phone in the living room. My dad is at the pub so you'll be all right there."

He hovered uneasily and then withdrew. The fire in the living room was banked up behind an old curved fire-guard. In front of it was a hand-pegged rug like the one she had bought. He had said his grandmother made rugs like that. The three-piece suite was stacked with hand-embroidered cushions. The pictures on the walls were like those she had discarded from the frames at the auction. The room belonged to a world she thought no longer existed. But for the large new TV and the modern coffee table, it could have been a room in her grandparents' home and she almost expected to find an old fretwork-fronted wireless somewhere. She rang Jessica's number, with an uneasy feeling.

"Jess?"

"Mum. Where have you been?"

"I've been painting."

"But I've been calling you. You've had your phone off."

"Sorry darling. I can't get a signal. It's the fells…. I mean, mountains."

"I wanted to talk to you."

Polly felt a sudden clutch of apprehension. "Mum. I'm not feeling very well," she heard. She balanced on the arm of the sofa ready to hear a familiar story. It is fine for children to leave home, she thought, - that is normal - but not for parents to do so, even for three months!

"What is it darling?"

"I don't know Mum. I just don't feel well."

Jessica frequently complained about not feeling well. Polly had stopped imagining what might be the problem, M.E. being her main fear, but in the past year she had felt wearied by her daughter's self-preoccupation. She needs a boyfriend, she would say to Brian. Yet Jessica's lack of confidence and resultant moodiness seemed designed to repel the possibilities. Of course Polly blamed herself for her daughter's weaknesses. If she had been more of a domestic mother and less of a "prima donna", as Brian called her whenever her absorption in work annoyed him, then maybe Jessica would be free of problems.

"What symptoms? You must have some symptoms."

"Not really. I just don't feel well."

"Are you getting to college?"

"Not today."

"Yesterday?"

"Yes, but I came home."

"Can you give me anything more to go on?"

"Not really. I just….."

Polly was beginning to get the measure of her daughter's mood. "….don't feel well," she finished for her.

"I knew you'd understand."

Now she would have to guess. That was the way the game was played. Had anything brought this on, how was College work going, was she missing her best friend, what about the French boyfriend, was she making new friends, how was the room she was living in turning out, did she see much of Brian's colleague, what about the guy upstairs? All questions brought a negative response.

"I'm supposed to go to Clare's wedding," Jessica offered at the end of the inquisition.

"And you don't want to go?"

"Not really"

"But you were so excited about it"

"That's 'was.' I thought I might go to France for a week"

"Instead?"

"No now."

"What now? It's term time, Jessica."

"I knew you'd say that."

Polly began to piece it together. Jessica had come back at the end of the summer term flushed with excitement at having fallen in love. There was a photograph of a dark-haired young man in loose fitting clothes. 'It's a start', Polly had said to Brian.

"Not much of one," he shrugged, "and why a bloody Frenchman?"

This conversation took place the morning after Jessica had moved into her bed-sit for the autumn term. Polly remembered it now, as it was the same day that she and Tom had inspected the flat overlooking the Thames. She had felt guilty at the comparison of style and space and cost between the two. Now she noted that memories of Tom invaded most things.

"Why can't she be like other students of her age? Why move only just around the corner, for heaven's sake," she'd complained.

"It's cheap and you are too hard on her," Brian had said, "just because she hasn't your confidence."

Brian's usual defence of Jessica made her think now that he could better help her as he was only down the road. She wasn't ill.

"Have you talked to your father?"

"Of course not."

"Why not?"

"He's moody and bad tempered, that's why."

This was probably Jessica's judgement on her for leaving Brian on his own! How would she behave if she really knew why Polly had come and what her life had been like the last year. Brian's moods and tempers could not be construed as justifying her affair with Tom - it needed no justification - but his air of despondency had done nothing to hold her.

"When are you coming back?" Jessica was asking.

"Like I told you, around Easter."

"Why not now?"

"The weather has only just started to improve so today is the first day I've got out to paint properly. This is not a holiday, Jess. I have to produce something. Your father knows that very well."

"Can I come up and see you?"

"It's still term time."

Her daughter's protest fizzled out. "You need to get a warm drink and go to bed. If you're feeling no better in the morning, go and see the doctor".

"OK Mum, I love you."

"I love you too," Polly replied, trying to keep a note of irritation from her voice.

Jessica grunted.

"I tell you what," Polly offered, " I'll get a telephone installed. Would that help?"

"A bit."

The conversation ended. So she had now agreed to have a telephone installed and she sighed before making her way back into the kitchen. The young man was watching a small television on the kitchen counter. He jumped up and switched it off.

"My mum says it's rude to leave it on when you have visitors," he said in explanation.

On the kitchen table, instead of the shoe-cleaning tins and brushes, was a crude painting of Mellbreak. The strange thing was that it was the same view she had been drawing all day.

"That's one of yours is it?"

"That's right. That's….. "

"….Mellbreak," she finished for him. "I've been there today"

He was pleased. "What d' you think of it?" adding quickly "I mean Mellbreak," in case she thought he had meant his painting which he was too shy to ask her about.

"I think it is very promising," referring to his work.

"Promising eh? What does that mean then?"

She hesitated and then said she thought he had caught the atmosphere of the place and that the colours were really good. He asked what would have made it better. Everyone should paint what they saw, she said, and that was different from what others saw. He should decide what he saw and make sure that is what he painted.

"Mellbreak's like a mistake somehow when everything else is bigger and smoother," he explained.

"That's very interesting," Polly said appreciatively.

"Can I come and see what you've done with it?"

Polly was not keen to be "the art teacher". She wanted to be left to paint.

"I haven't really started it yet," she replied, non-committally.

"When you have?"

"OK, when I have."

That might stall the curiosity of this raw young man. She made to leave but at that point the back door opened and Ethel came in and put down her basket on the kitchen table beside the painting. Polly felt momentarily embarrassed as if Ethel had interrupted something.

"Oh. Oh….so here you are," said Ethel stopping in her tracks…"how do you do, *Mrs* Creed, is it? You've met my son Jonty?"

Polly nodded. "An unusual name."

"Not round these parts, he said.

"Call me Polly, please," she said.

"Mrs Creed, I mean Polly," said Jonty blushing, "came to make a phone-call"

"Yes, it was your daughter. Is everything all right?"

"Oh yes, I think so." Polly was eager to convey motherliness.

"How old is she?

"Nineteen."

"Missing you I expect? Sometimes they take a long time to grow away, " said Ethel meaningfully.

Jonty looked at his feet and Ethel looked at his painting.

"You've not wasted your time then," she said to him sharply, "taking up Mrs Creed's time. What d' you think, Mrs Creed?"

Polly noticed that Ethel did not use her first name and guessed she was thereby sending a message to Jonty. Polly repeated that she thought his work was interesting.

"Work, you see, Mum. She called it work."

"Not what your father calls work," said Ethel turning to Polly, "Everything all right at the barn? Anything you want?"

"No, well yes… is there any objection to my getting a telephone installed so I don't have to bother you again? "

"It's no bother."

She explained that Jessica was very insistent that she might want to get hold of her sometimes and that her mobile didn't work here. She launched into an unnecessary explanation that she had not wanted to bring her computer here so could not be e-mailed either.

"You do that, then do you, that e-mail?" said Ethel.

"Yes, for my work."

"Well, we leave that to Jonty."

"Is a telephone all right then?"

"As long as it's made out to you and is disconnected when you leave."

" Of course."

Polly made her way out clumsily through a succession of doors into the farmyard. She had just lost something of her privacy without meaning to do so. She had also spoken to so few people since arriving in the village that she seemed to have lost the knack of ordinary conversation. Not that this village was ordinary for her - even the mention of computers drew attention to its difference. She heard cows nearby shuffle in the darkness, smelling the sweet, milky earthiness that she was coming to recognise. She jumped when a farm dog pushed his nose into her hand and felt a clutch of panic to get out of the yard and back to her room, afraid of the dark as if she were some city child on a farm holiday. She stepped swiftly into the village street, her boots making a clatter on the tarmac. The sunshine of the day had dried up the usual puddles and there was frost on the hedges and ice on the road. There were no street-lights but when the moon emerged over the fells, it created a world of white brilliance. That would be Knock Murton, she thought, pleased to know its name.

*   *   *

Brian was brooding about McNally. He might hold him off for a while but in the end he was on the modernist winning side. He was glad Polly now had a phone even though they agreed only to speak on Sundays but he decided not to tell Polly about McNally when she next rang him. She would read between the lines and see what Max was trying to do. Max was impressed by her and she knew it.

The next day he had a visit from McNally in his office.

"Brian, can I have a word?"

Can he have a word? The same opening as Max. Ron McNally was in his thirties. He had taught for a short time before becoming a lecturer in education, something that he believed distinguished him as a man with a mission whereas Brian thought it left him splashing about in the shallows, misunderstanding children. Ron thought children learned best if they had clear targets whereas Brian believed that children wanted to learn and your job was not to hinder them. That was now called 'old Sixties stuff'. Ron on the contrary was blowing along with the prevailing wind, bambouzling Max into the bargain. He had often said as much to Polly but she had sighed and said, "Oh, let it alone Brian."

"Well, Ron. I gather you want my help," he began in jocular style, which was feebly aimed to put Ron onto the wrong foot.

"Brian, of course, yes, yes I do..." Ron rubbed the designer stubble on his chin.

"In what way can an old lag like myself help you?" He knew at once his hostility was showing through.

"Well, it's your support really....."

"Oh my support. So you don't want my views, I take it?"

"No, no that's not what I mean, of course not..."

Brian waited a good few seconds, maximising the younger man's discomfort. He was not so sure of himself after all. Becoming brisk, Brian made the next move, like a craftily angled service in a tennis match.

'What *exactly* have you been asked to do?"

"Well," Ron replied, his picture of what a review actually entailed visibly disappearing and clearly not wanting to get into a wrangle, "to review the whole syllabus".

"Ah," nodded Brian, "to review the whole syllabus.... I see..."

"And teaching styles."

"Ah yes, Max said as much. How do you plan to do that then?"

A fruitless discussion ensued with the only outcome that Ron McNally offered to show Brian a draft of how he intended to proceed with the Review. Both men were bruised by the encounter.

*   *   *

While washing her hair one morning, Polly recalled the start of the affair. She had been sorting out students' paintings for assessment, dragging canvases across the floor to get a full look at them. It was late in the evening and she switched off the lights as she came out. And there he was standing across the corridor. There was no-one else about. She knew at once that he had been waiting for her. Because she had been lugging things about, her hair had fallen over her eyes. To her surprise, he stepped right up to her and stroked the hair away from her face. The skin on her face and neck had tingled. He said he had been passing and caught sight of her through the glass panel of the door. Would she join him for a drink in the bar. Her hesitation encouraged him to go further, to cup her chin in his hands and confidently brush a kiss on her lips.

"What are you doing?" she whispered.

"What I have been thinking of doing for a week or two. Now seemed as good a time as any."

His audacity took her breath away. Had she known, hoped, it would come to that?

"You're not going anywhere else are you?"

"No, but I usually…."

"This is not usual, believe you me. I recognised something about you and me from the start. Didn't you? Be honest."

So she let herself be taken by the elbow out of the side door of the College into a taxi and into town and to a restaurant, with candles, with quiet waiters, with an atmosphere that encouraged her to stay in the trance that he had induced in her. She went home reeling, forced to invent a story about why she was so much later than usual and had arrived in a taxi.

And then, of course, it happened again, but this time by arrangement. At the end of the next meal, it was clear that an affair was to follow. He took her to a friend's empty flat and they made love in a borrowed bed. The next time, he told her he had acquired a flat. She went with him to view it and they made love on their coats on the unfurnished shining wooden floor. It was in the dockland area and afterwards they stood looking out over the Thames from its high, narrow balcony. It was entirely private and soon became their trysting place. When they could be free, they spent the afternoons choosing furniture, eventually ending up on the mattress of a smart bed as soon as it was delivered.

He hung her painting over the bed to celebrate, he said. The flat was spacious and minimalist and made her too feel spacious and liberated from the daily details of her life. For at least one evening a week, she would stay there until ten o'clock, often arriving back in Fern Road at the same time as Brian, who had taken somehow to working later and later. On that bed, soon covered in clouds of white cotton, they discussed College politics, national politics, music, his life and hers, about his ambitions and her painting. The daze of excitement was increased by their complicity. She felt like an exotic plant that had been long in need of water now flowering in a secret location. And a life-time of organisational skills came to her aid, equipping her to run a double life.

Ironically, the sheer minimalism of their love-nest made her final visit relatively simple as there was no tell-tale clutter to clear away.

*   *   *

She was deep in this reverie when there was a knock on the door. It was Veronica.

"I hope I am not intruding but I was in the churchyard and…..

"Come in, please"

Polly was very glad to see her. "I'll make some coffee. Do sit down – no, over there."

She placed her guest in the oak chair. The sun was shining directly onto the rug beside it and the sheen of the chair and the glowing colours of the rug made an island of colour.

"The rug is beautiful," said Veronica

"I bought it at the auction. I couldn't resist it. Jonty helped me to get it home together with that lamp and some picture frames."

Veronica paused before saying, "I hope I am not interfering but you might want to be a bit careful with Jonty."

"Really?"

"He doesn't meet many young women hereabouts these days."

"But I am years older."

"He may not know that."

"He knows I have a grown-up daughter."

"Good," Veronica said, quickly changing the subject. "Well, that is not why I came of course. I came in the hope that I might see your painting?"

"Of course."

Polly moved 'Mellbreak' into the light. She had been working hard at it but it was not coming right. Veronica rose stiffly from her chair to look at it from different angles and distances.

"It looks dark and bright at the same time with blocks of strong colour contrasting with the grey–blue of the sky," she pronounced eventually, "making it stand out from the canvas as if it were coming out of it and the light seems to be shining from inside. "

Polly was pleased with her response and made the coffee.

Veronica continued. " I see what you mean about mountains and secrets. It has a mysterious depth, as if there is life inside it. Yes," she said, clapping her hands together," almost as if it were the mountain the Pied Piper led the children dancing into. Is that too fanciful?"

Polly laughed. "I didn't know it could tell a story."

"Ah" said Veronica.

Painting Mellbreak had indeed become an emotional business for Polly. Tom had been in her mind most of the time. And now the temptation to share some of her story suddenly became very great. She passed her new friend the mug of coffee.

"I will light the fire, shall I?" thinking partly of her visitor's age. "It is rather cold here. And then, drawing back from her impulse to confess her own situation, she switched the focus. " Perhaps you can tell me a bit more about yourself in exchange for the viewing?"

Veronica smiled and returned to the chair to watch Polly put the sticks and paper into the stove, light it and arrange the logs."

"Do you collect your own logs?

Polly said that she enjoyed collecting wood, especially when the rain cleared in the late afternoons and drops of water lit up the cobwebs and the Old Man's Beard straggling the hedges.

"Ah" said Veronica" you are falling under the spell.'

Polly sat down opposite her, noticing with approval her fine wool suit and elegant boots. Veronica began her story.

"If you look out of your barn window up there, to the right, you will see where I was born - in an old house on that moor eighty years ago. My father was a doctor just as my husband, a generation later. He always said that driving home from the coastal towns through these hedgerows at the end of the day was like putting on a clean shirt. "

"How did you meet your husband?"

"Long story. I will make it short. I was not a well child and our house was cold and isolated, and a long way from the village school, so my mother arranged for me and my sister to take lessons with the two boys at the big house nearby belonging to a Mr Osbert Cornfrew, the owner of one of the Whitehaven pits. The miners of course lived in the towns which is why the old man chose to live a good distance away from them and he didn't want his sons mixing with town children, mining children, nor village boys, come to that." She paused. "Robert was one of the Cornfrew sons. It is the Cornfrew grave just outside the church door. We grew up together until he went up to Cambridge to read medicine." She stopped and seemed to pull herself up short. The war broke out, he enlisted and was gone."

And she put down her cup and stood up, drawing on her soft leather gloves. Polly was disappointed not to be told more. She realized she had her own reasons for wanting to hear more and also pulled back.

"Would you let me paint you?" she asked on impulse.

Veronica turned to her in surprise.

"Me? I am not the beauty I fancied I once was!" she laughed.

"But I think you would make a good subject."

"Why, might I ask?"

"You are somewhat, well, mysterious."

Chapter Four

BBC North West Television Breakfast News.

'On Wednesday, February 21st, sheep that had passed through Longtown Livestock Market on February 15th were diagnosed with foot and mouth disease. It was suspected that the infection might have come from a pig sent to Essex from near Newcastle. The virus was identified as the pan Asiatic O type strain.'

February 21st 2001

There was a frown on his mother's face when Jonty came in from milking.

"You'd better watch this," she said, flapping her hand at the television in the kitchen.

Jim followed him in and the three of them stood watching the local breakfast news. When the account of the outbreak of Foot and Mouth in Longtown finished, he and Jonty sat down for their breakfast in silence while Ethel moved about uneasily behind them.

"It'll not get here,' said Jim.

Almost immediately the telephone rang. Ethel answered it.

"It's your brother," she said, handing Jim the phone.

Jonty's uncle, his father's younger brother, Eric, farmed over near the Scottish border. By agreement between the brothers, and according to the will of their father, Jim had taken over in Milnethwaite and Eric had rented a small farm in Northumberland soon after their father died.

"It'll not come to that," they heard him say," not these days," before putting down the phone. He sat down again with a humph.

"It'll not get here," he said again, without looking at them.

"What'd he say?" urged Ethel.

Jonty suspected a crisis by his father's face yet knew he wasn't going to tell them what he'd heard. He had a way of dismissing bad news when it first hit him. Jonty however had known about

54

the last outbreak all his life as his father had described it in detail many times over.

" He bought fifteen in-lamb ewes at Longtown sheep market last week," he said tersely. "It'll be bound to be handled better than the 1967 lot, you mark my words.

*　　　　　*　　　　　*

"Isn't that near where your Mum is?" said Sue, Miles's girlfriend.
Miles and Sue were sitting on the sofa in Sue's flat watching the ten o'clock news. They had eaten an Indian take-away. Miles was watching Sue admiringly as she curled long strands of her blond hair around her fingers.

"Well, she's up in the north-west somewhere."

"Don't you know where she is?" Sue came from Leeds and was in London on a short-term government contract. Miles had met her at a conference on IT development.

"Not really."

"You don't know anything about the north at all do you?"

"Not much. I only think about it when you are there and I try not to think about it then." He threw a cushion at her. Sue had a young son and a husband whom she saw only at weekends.

"Well, I tell you Longtown is in Cumbria and that's where your Mum is."

"So what?"

"Foot and Mouth can be serious, Miles."

"People don't catch it do they?"

"Miles Creed! You are an ignorant townie, a southerner and middle class and everything I don't like!"

Miles and Sue had been spending time together for well over a year. He had been mightily impressed by her presentation at that conference. She was confident with her material that involved the mapping of welfare benefits take-up in the streets of Leeds. But he was more impressed by her confidence in herself. The women he met at work and on his journeys to and from work were pretty routine-looking - same hairstyles, same clothes, same kinds of conversations. He was beginning to despair of meeting anyone more interesting. But he had managed to sit beside her over lunch and found her glad to talk as she knew no-one having just arrived in the city. She was exceedingly attractive and unself-conscious – easy and exciting company for a fellow like him. He had arranged to show her the sights and this had led onto more lunches, then suppers and so to visiting his flat and to his amazement, sleeping with him. It had never been so easy for him before and yet she was married and had a child. They didn't talk about that much. After all it was all very temporary.

*   *   *

Brian woke up in the arm-chair with a stiff neck just as the ten o'clock news was coming to an end and the newsreader was repeating the main headlines. There was a foot and mouth outbreak in Cumbria. Polly would have her head in the clouds and probably never even listened to the news. She was near the West coast anyway and this was in the North East. He pulled himself up out of the chair to look at the map and found Longtown and Carlisle and then, eventually, Milnethwaite. She should be all right and if it got bad it might bring her back early. Evenings, like the one he had just slept through, were the worst times.

*   *   *

Jessica phoned her father to say that she was not feeling well. He suggested she came in for a drink. He mentioned the outbreak of foot and mouth but she took no account of it.

"It might bring her home, " he said, adding quickly, "and I'm thinking you might be missing her."

"Are you then?" she asked at once.

"Apart from the fact that I might be drinking too much whisky, not much, as she was usually out in the evenings when she was here."

"And you were in?"

"Fair point! As an artist and, I might dare to say even to you, a woman, she somehow avoided having to run a department."

"You sound like a real male dinosaur!"

He grunted and then laughed.

"Perhaps I am, so you'd better let me take you out for a meal to keep me from extinction!"

*　　　　　*　　　　　*

As he left for the fields, Jonty didn't know how to react to the news. Although he didn't remember the 1967 epidemic, he'd grown up to think of it as a disaster still looming over their lives. Since then there'd been the Chernobyl cloud of radio-activity that had landed on the fells and put a stop to the sale of lambs for a few years. Then Mad Cow disease had arrived to call a halt to the sale of beef. Not surprisingly, Jim had passed onto him a doom-laden view of fell-farming. His father was getting old. His lungs had been damaged by a lifetime of farming and his weariness made him irritable and reactionary. If they were to be caught up in a new epidemic his father would add to disaster by resisting help and criticising everyone else.

In his gloom, Jonty happened to be going through the field behind the church. He needed something to cheer him up, so he'd just stop at Church Terrace to tell Polly the news.

*　　　　　*　　　　　*

Polly turned off the Today programme at nine o'clock on hearing a knock at the door. She found Jonty standing awkwardly screwing up his cap.

"Good smelling coffee," he said so she reluctantly beckoned him to come inside.

"Want some?" she waved the coffee-pot in his direction.

"Did my mum leave you that coffee-pot?"

" I brought it with me. I need the buzz in the mornings."
The thought of her needing a 'buzz' excited him and he watched her toss her hair from her face to pour the coffee.

"I wonder you don't get paint in your hair, it's that long."

"Is the foot and mouth serious, do you think?" she asked ignoring his comment.

"Ah, you've heard."

"Just, yes."

"Too early to tell. My dad doesn't think it'll get here though my uncle must be dead worried as he bought some sheep from that market at the time of the infection, if you heard that on the news. "

"Will it make any difference to you?"

"We might get a few restrictions in travel, I suppose," he said, thinking that if he said the right thing, it might keep her up here or if he said the wrong thing, make her leave.

 "Well, what have you come for?" she asked, handing him his coffee.

"Mellbreak," he grinned.
So, without enthusiasm, she spread some drawings across the table and uncovered the canvas on the easel, wishing she hadn't let him in.

After a confused pause, he muttered, "it isn't much like Mellbreak and yet it is."

"That's good news then," she said cheerily.
He then looked up the stairs in the direction of the bedroom.

"I used to play up there. You know – where your bed is."

"Did you?"

"I did that. Comfy bed I bet. Used to be straw up there."☐
He was large and loomed over her. He had a pleasant face, she supposed, with a ruddy complexion and tufts of light brown hair, sticking out at angles as a result of the pressure of the cap he always seemed to wear. Unsurprisingly, he smelt of the farmyard. After a long silence, which she refused to break and in which he shifted awkwardly about, he thanked her for the coffee, carefully

placing his mug on the counter, and left. She shivered with relief as she had become a little wary of him.

Restrictions on travel might affect her then, she reflected. She might either be expected to leave or forced to stay. But she knew at once that it was imperative that she stay.

*   *   *

February 22nd 2001: BBC Radio Four News
> '*An outbreak of foot and mouth has been declared and a seven-day ban announced on all animal movements of cattle, pigs, sheep and goats. 25,000 sheep had passed through Longtown Livestock Market between 14th and 23rd of February. The whole of Great Britain is declared a controlled area*'

The day after the announcement was another wet West Cumbrian morning. The bus stopped in Milnethwaite and Ethel, the last out, found Alice waiting for her, offering a share of her old umbrella with a bent spoke. Ethel shook off the offer.

"Jim'll be worried," began Alice, "about this foot and mouth business."

"Not as yet," said Ethel briskly, knowing Alice's predilection for bad news.

"Well, ain't Jim's brother up near Carlisle?"

"He is," said Ethel.

"They say it's spread by the Longtown market up there."

"They do," said Ethel definitively.

"Well, that's near him, ain't it?"

"It is."

Alice made a low, wondering sound and sniffed as if nothing more were needed to put Jim and Ethel at the centre of the drama. Ethel began to move off, but Alice wasn't finished yet.

"Your Jonty's taking his painting serious these days, so they say."

"Not as I'm aware of," said Ethel

"Maybe *you're* not," said Alice as if everyone else but Ethel knew something. "Going to get his own teacher, so they say."

"Do they now," said Ethel grimly, "Some haven't got enough to occupy them in my view."

"Just what I said," said Alice.

"I'll be on my way Alice," said Ethel," It's raining quite hard now."

She left Alice standing. Alice shrugged and set off down the lane holding her umbrella firmly against the driving rain.

"Jonty," Ethel called, as she shook off her mackintosh and hung it up on the back door, muttering "damned woman."

"I'm in the living room." Jonty had his pictures out again on the table

"Put those away while I get dinner," said Ethel impatiently, "and keep them out of your Dad's way and all. Old Alice's got her sights on you and the painter lady."

*   *   *

On Thursday evening, Miles and Sue were standing on the crowded Victoria Line tube train having scrambled on at Euston. It was a wet evening and the rush hour was even more of a crush than usual. Seeing the foot and mouth news on the hoardings, Sue raised her voice above the low commuter hum.

"Tell me again, why she is up there?"

"To paint." Miles was embarrassed at having to raise his voice.

"What sort of painting?"

"Abstracts."

"Why the Lake District if she does abstracts?"

"Well, perhaps she gets them from scenes," Miles said irritably as heads turned in his direction.

They got seats when the train emptied at Finchley Road and Sue snuggled up to him.

"Is her painting any good?"

"People seem to think so."

"I'd like to meet her."

"You nearly did."

Miles then told her, in a low voice, how he had seen his mother when they were in Soho. She was with some bloke, probably a colleague, he said.

"Why didn't you introduce me?"

"I didn't want her to see you."

"Why not?"

Miles looked uncomfortable.

"Because I'm married?" Sue said and then, "perhaps she didn't want to see you!"

*   *   *

Jim heard the news at five thirty the next morning on 'Farming Today'. An official outbreak of foot and mouth had been declared. A seven-day ban had been announced on all animal movements of cattle, pigs, sheep and goats.

"Only animals already on the move are allowed to complete their journeys, so, as I said, we'll be all right," Jim said to Jonty as he joined him later in the sheds. "They had it coming. Too many farmers are moving their beasts all over the country to get to auctions and slaughter-houses. It's a crazy way to farm."

Back in the kitchen for breakfast, he picked up the Cumberland News as it dropped in the letterbox and read out the leading paragraph to Ethel and Jonty over breakfast

' 25,000 sheep have passed through Longtown Livestock Market between 14th and 23rd of February – a number described as unprecedented.'

"Fancy allowing all that movement!" he grunted, "This government learns nothing. Read the rest out, Jonty, I haven't got my specs handy."

Jonty read on:

The whole of Great Britain is declared a controlled area and footpaths might soon have to be closed. The Minister, Nick Brown, confirmed that pigs on Burnside Farm, Heddon-on-the-wall, were thought to be the source and had probably been infected via swill. He described the outbreak as

'absolutely terrible.'

"What does he know about farming!" Jim growled. "Go on."

'The government had acted with exemplary speed.'

"Not fast enough in my opinion,*"* said Jim.

"Am I reading this or not!" Jonty resumed impatiently.

' Ben Gill of the National Farmers' Union is advising farmers to 'batten down the hatches. All farmers who have no choice but to have their animals slaughtered will be compensated at the full market value. Ministry vets and officials are to visit within a two-mile radius of those placed under exclusion measures to see if the disease had spread'.

"There you are, said Jim," as he grabbed the paper back and smacked it shut "What did I tell you? It'll be like 1967 all over again!"

"You said nothing of the sort," said Ethel. "You said it'd all be different this time."

Jonty said "Longtown. We all know that's uncle's area!"

"That's as maybe,' said Jim, "but it won't get as far as here. Not if we're careful."

The advice of the NFU representative over the phone the day before had been to watch Ministry news on the computer rather than waiting for BBC bulletins or the newspapers.

"We'll have to get the computer going," Jim said. "That's a job for you, Jonty lad. No more going to market and picking up fancy women. Everything'll be shut down now. You take note. I know. I've seen it all afore." He stumped out slamming the door behind him.

Jonty slowly ate his porridge. His father had never wanted the computer in the house but the NFU man insisted.

"You have to get linked up Jim," he'd said. " Keep up with the times."

"I don't need to be linked up with anyone, thank you," his father had grunted.

"Well, for Jonty here's sake. When he takes over, it'll be essential."

"That'll be a long time coming."

The NFU man had winked at Jonty. "I know about fathers and sons in farms hereabouts," he'd said. "Don't hang on too long or he'll be off to work in a garage in town, eh Jonty, like all the others."

"Over my dead body," muttered Jim.

"Indeed, indeed. It might be too." The man shook his head and left with no further comment.

His father was like an old dog; any new smell and he'd pee on it! He went into the living room where the computer had been installed. It was covered in its plastic cover. It wasn't even plugged in. He began to connect it up, hoping he would remember how to start it. He managed to switch it on and then tried to get onto the internet. All the time he was fiddling around with it, trying this and that, he was also thinking about Polly. She brought back all the old longings. He'd had no girl for months, years almost. Anyone he'd really fancied seemed to leave the area. Yet Polly was something different. She was dead classy and, boy, stunning to look at, especially close to. If he could only get to know her, she was someone he could talk to about something other than the usual farming stuff as well as….. already fantasies about painting her and her painting him got him to sleep at night. After all, she was here on her own. What could that mean? She had a daughter – he knew that – but she didn't talk about a husband. She was a modern sort of woman all right. She might be glad of a man if she was stuck up here. He had been thinking he might invite her to go out with him a few times, show her some places to paint, but, now, with all this going on, it was hard to make a move and he'd made a hash of it so far.

He suddenly connected with the fact that she'd told his mother she used email. He stopped day-dreaming, knowing just what to do. He switched off the computer, pushed his chair back very gently from the table, rose quietly and slipped out the back. His father was looking out for some old bits of carpet and sacking to soak in disinfectant to lay across the farm entrance. Bio-security, it was called. He made for Polly's barn without being seen.

*   *   *

Polly was coming down in her dressing gown after a shower and barely disguised her weariness when she found Jonty at the door.

"Sorry it's a bit early and it's not about painting this time. Can you work a computer?" he said.

"Of course. No-one in higher education can exist without doing so these days - even painters."

"Can you come and look at ours then? I can't make it work and I've got to get it going to find out the latest about this foot and mouth rubbish. It's urgent."

She couldn't refuse. "Yes of course. Just let me put some clothes on."

When she came down the stairs he was again fidgeting from one foot to another. He'd been in a state of excitement thinking of her up there, getting undressed and dressed.

"Do you mind kind of trying not to be seen? – it's me dad you see. He thinks I should be able to do it."

She felt unease as he guided her out of the yard across the cobbles and a soaking wet garden lawn to a French window at the back of the farmhouse.

"We won't be seen this way," he said, "Dad's sorting out the disinfectant and Mum's doing the hens and ducks. You'll have to take your shoes off."

She bent to do so and stumbled in the attempt. He steadied her with his hand. At the computer he helped her off with her coat. Pulling herself together she set to work.

"Do you think you can do it?"

"I'll try."

She tested all the connections, tightening up one or two, and clicked on to the internet but nothing happened. He was leaning forward to read the screen, his hand on her shoulder.

"I shall have to ring the Helpline. Have you the number?"

she said.

He looked nervously at his watch. The excitement of being in such close proximity to her was outweighed by the fear of being discovered by his mother. Fortunately the Helpline number was stuck on the computer so she went to the phone, also anxious not to get caught out in this clandestine operation. She dialled and waited what seemed a very long time while Jonty fidgeted.

"They've just changed the number – that's all, " she said. "You sit down and I will talk you through what to do."

She had no alternative but to lean over him to show him the keys to press. She could detect his creamy, milky smell realizing that he might well also smell her shower gel. When at last connected, he stood, clapped his hands and clasped both her hands just as his mother walked in. They both sprang apart.

"You're sorting out that thing between you, I see," Ethel said severely, seeing the flush on Jonty's face with obvious alarm.

Jonty, following Polly's advice, now connected the computer to the MAFF website and the three of them watched the headline information come up. They read that when the first case had been confirmed, 57 farms in 16 counties were already affected. Tracing the contacts from Longtown was to be a long job. Compensation was to be awarded to those farmers whose animals had to be slaughtered.

"That's where Jim's brother'll be for it, no question," said Ethel.

"But happen he'll be better off for the compensation than the rest of us" said Jonty. "We'll get no grants or compensation. We'll have to buy our own bio-security and we'll sell nothing now except milk and that might be stopped soon. Look," he said pointing to the screen, "the cattle markets are all shut down."

"It would break your uncle's heart to have his animals slaughtered no matter what the price – and Jim's too."

"Should I leave the barn, do you think?" Polly asked Ethel.

"That's up to you, Mrs Creed. I won't let the place out afresh if you go, not now, but you can stay as far as I'm concerned, if you've a mind to, that is."

There was a double edge to Ethel's voice.

"Perhaps it would all be over by Easter, do you think, when I intended to leave anyway?"

"I hope so."

"Can I be of help if I stay?" she asked.

"That's very kind of you," said Ethel. She paused. "I suppose, you might do me a bit of shopping now and then and leave it at the gate. We can't go into town for fear of bringing contamination in but you should be all right if you stick to the main roads. We can't go calling on you from now on, nor you on us any more," firmly looking at Jonty.

Polly was beginning to read Ethel. She was brusque in manner and straight-forward and she liked that.

*   *   *

On his journey to work, Miles wondered about Sue's comment that his mother might not have wanted to be seen that night in town. Their mutual silence about their sighting had puzzled him. He'd like to come clean and tell her about Sue. He'd call Jess for his mother's new number, which he'd lost, when he got into the office.

"What d'you want to talk to her about then?" Jessica demanded, predictably.

"Nothing in particular."

"Have you got a girl friend at last and want to reassure her you're not gay."

"Jess! I'm at work. Someone might hear."

"Well then. Have you?"

"I might have."

"Can I meet her?"

"No."

"Why not?"

"Never you mind."

"Is she married or something then?"

"Be quiet." Miles hissed, appalled that she had guessed the truth.

"She is then!"

"I never said so."

"Exactly. I'm not stupid. You're a lousy liar. You know that?"

"Leave it, Jess."

"Want to tell Mummy about your triumph or is it problems, is that it?"

"Shut up Jess. Just give me her number. I have a perfect right to talk to my mother if I choose."

"I'm right aren't I? You're having an affair! Is it one of your office chicks?"

"No, she is not." He'd now given away more than he had intended. " I can't talk like this. I'm in the office. Will you give me her number or not."

"OK. OK. She's just had a telephone put in where she is. There's no network coverage for the mobile as she is stuck behind mountains apparently." She gave him the number. "Say thank you!"

*　　　　　　*　　　　　　*

On Friday evening, Brian met Jessica at an Indian restaurant near the College. It was early in the evening. He watched her as she came into the restaurant to join him at a table in the window. She moved without confidence. She was only a little like Polly; not the same energy in her step. More like him in many ways. She was not as attractive to men as Polly either. It was strange looking at her when she had yet not caught sight of him. He recalled her as a young child. He had been overwhelmed with love for her. She had been bright, pert and talented all through school. But now she seemed as if she were operating on half power. Had she got this dreaded ME? Was she afraid of failing her course? Was she really in love? At least he could try to be a decent father and find out, especially if Polly was taking a sabbatical from motherhood as well as from everything else.

Jessica on the other hand, had but one thought in her mind - her suspicions about Miles. She was sure he had a secret and that she had hit upon the right answer. She strongly disapproved of affairs. They were always damaging to someone, though she was at the same time mildly impressed that Miles might actually be taking such a risk. She wanted to take more risks herself but was alarmed that Miles might be stupid enough to get entangled in someone else's marriage. She wouldn't tell tales on him, certainly not to her stuffy father, but she wouldn't be doing that if she just raised the possibility. Miles had actually told her nothing but she was sure something was going on. She'd kind of work it into the conversation and test out her father's reaction. She could then warn Miles about how to play it.

It was the first meal ever alone together and was rather strained. Both skirted around what they had intended to say. They exchanged a few comments about Polly and the Foot and Mouth epidemic, aware that they each might be feeling similarly abandoned by her.

Brian voiced his own concerns first, thinking thereby to encourage her to open up about hers. He told her about the departmental review and that he might be considered too old and staid. He was of course asking for reassurance and got it. Jessica was touched that he had confided in her. When she knew that he hadn't told Polly, she was even more impressed and proceeded to take a serious interest. He warmed to her wholehearted approval of his approach to education. She was delighted to see him cheer up and he found watching her immensely pleasurable as she became animated in his defence. They drank more wine, enjoying the novelty of their new relationship. Eventually he asked her about herself. Was her course going satisfactorily? Could he help her to plan out her work as he did for his students? Was she missing her mother? Had he been too abrupt in turning down her suggestion of returning home for the revision term? To all of these questions she said "Nope" but eventually confided, as with Polly a few nights ago, her impulse to go to France and seek out

Pierre. Brian looked studiously concerned and then so relieved when she said she had decided to stick at the course that she laughed aloud.

"You should see your face! A daughter of yours, giving up her course and running off to France! What would that say about your role as the guru-father figure in the education department!"
He laughed a little uncomfortably.

"I told Mum and she gave me the old 'Get on with your life' stuff too."
He said he was glad she had telephoned Polly and asked how she thought she was.

"Don't you two talk?" Jessica sat back in her chair and looked at him disapprovingly.

"Only on Sunday evenings by agreement. We agreed to leave her to her own devices to get on with her work."

At last Jessica raised her suspicion about Miles. Could he have a girlfriend at last? Brian said he had never divulged anything about Polly to his family until they were actually engaged. He thought that if Miles were to tell anyone it would be Polly.

"He was very secretive and defensive about it," Jessica said.

"Leave him to sort it out, Jess. He'll tell us anything he wants us to know when he's ready."
He asked for the bill to stone-wall any more hints, emptied the bottle of wine into their glasses and looked at his watch. Jessica continued undeterred.

"What if she were married?" Jessica said this slowly with whispered drama leaning over the tablecloth.

"No," said Brian in a matter of fact way. "He wouldn't do that. Not Miles."

"Why not?"

"He's like me – a conventional lad! Not a romancer like you."

"Times change Dad." Jessica was luring him.

He humored her. "What makes you think it?"

"I said she might be married and he asked for Mum's

telephone number."

"Is that all?" He sat back laughing, to Jessica's annoyance, and then rose to leave. "How's your landlord?" changing the subject to his divorced colleague. "Is he missing his wife?"

"He keeps on talking about how he never knew she was committing adultery."

"How can anyone just not know?" he said.

As he put the car in the garage he decided to invite both his children round for a Sunday lunch.

*　　　　　　*　　　　　　*

On March 6th, Polly heard the official announcement that all footpaths were now closed. Though the virus was not yet into West Cumbria, this put paid to her planned painting trips. She'd been here for little over a month and had practically nothing to show for it. Into her hideaway had come this unforeseeable intrusion. She was as urban as it was possible to be and yet she was in the remotest part of England, shut off by mountains, in a village where there were more cows than people, where the people were a mystery to her and all were now consumed by a crisis. On the one hand, there was Jonty screwing up his cap, harbouring fantasies about a painting career and goodness knows what else and on the other, Alice, following her every move around the village with unconcealed curiosity.

What could she possibly do that could be of any interest to anyone here? She was spent and empty. Whenever it rained, and it rained very often indeed, it was as much as she could do to get through a day and she was totally failing to get through a night without lying awake tired and distressed. Was her grief abnormal in some way? How and when could she expect to be free of it? Yet at the same time as wanting to be free of it she knew she was clutching it to herself to preserve Tom from the distance opening up between them. If she were ever to be free of it, to let herself be free of it, she would have to face a future without him.

She sighed as she thought of that ……and of Brian. They

had become so distant and their times together were suffused with unacknowledged tension. Neither of them ever opened a discussion about their relationship – he had never done that all the time they were married and she had resisted doing so for fear that she would end up having to tell him about Tom.

As for her painting, apart from one stunningly beautiful day by Loweswater, the only sparks of inspiration came in the rare days when the weather cleared. As a result, the painting was no longer going well and the remorseless rain intensified her despair. If she could no longer drive out to see or work on Mellbreak, what would she have to show for her time here that would be seen to justify it?

Her thoughts then turned to Veronica who was coming for her first sitting. She very much wanted to paint her. A portrait was not the great work of mountains she had envisaged but might capture something about the mood of the place, even perhaps its current air of suspense. She was an enigmatic woman, having found a fulfilling love late in life only to lose it again. And maybe she would find some answers herself in the process.

*   *   *

The Vice-Chancellor phoned Brian.

"You knew Tom Frost as well as anyone Brian," he began.

"I guess so." Brian was quite pleased at this.

"We need his room. Can you collect his stuff and take it to his wife, do you think?"

Brian telephoned Marjorie Frost straightaway to avoid putting the call off simply because it was going to be difficult and arranged a visit. He went to Tom's office to collect the remainder of his working life here – a few photographs stacked against the wall, a mackintosh, several shelves of books and two big boxes of files apparently from his previous places of work. The College internal stuff from the filing cabinet must have gone elsewhere. There was clearly someone about to move in as there were two boxes dumped inside the door with 'Bradford University

Economics Department' labelled in felt tip pen. As he had suspected, this was indeed the expected invasion by the money boys. According to the Guardian, London was the capital of world finance and this was something in which we should apparently all rejoice. Well, not him! He only hoped his son in the city would keep his integrity.

Mrs Frost had given him travel instructions and he had printed off a map from the internet. He couldn't resist looking at the property prices in the area while printing the map. Tom would never have afforded property in that area on a professor's salary! Still, he had no quarrel with Tom and now the poor man was dead. He had a heavy job carting the stuff to his car and cursed the Vice-Chancellor for offering no practical help. Just flattery all the way! He set off for Surrey. He slowed down as he turned into the Frosts' road to find about ten large houses set at respectful distances from each other either side of the sandy road. Each was fronted by a paved courtyard with, obviously, a large area of garden at the back, richly planted with trees. Some houses had security gates and all had burglar alarms and neighbourhood watch notices in the windows. Number 12 boasted security gates, as he might have guessed, and he was impressed that they opened as he drove up. He looked at his watch. He was well on time. The house was of 1990s design, built by an expensive builder with a lot of smart detailing. The window surrounds and the doors were of good quality, recently treated wood. The walls were decorated with expensive brickwork, the whole beneath mock Tudor gables. There were bay trees in pots by the front door and contoured beds either side professionally planted, with flowering winter jasmine tailored along the walls.

He decided to go to the door before unloading. The bell was quickly answered by a middle-aged woman, smartly and conventionally dressed with neat, grey hair and a quiet manner. Her appearance reassured him that he should be able to cope; no excessive grief out of control. She politely asked him in for tea.

"I am very sorry to have to call for this reason," he began.

She smiled. "It is kind of you to go the trouble. I just

didn't feel quite able to get up into town myself."

"Of course, not, nor should you. You have suffered a great loss."

She greeted this remark with silence, but was more relaxed than he feared. In fact she seemed more at ease than he was, as she showed him in and took his coat.

"Your husband was a fine man," he ventured. "His death was a great loss to the College".

She waved her hand in a deprecating way. "My husband was a driven man," she replied.

"A great loss."

"He had his fingers in many pies," she said without acknowledging his sympathy. "I have been surprised to find how many."

"Gifted people often do." What did he know about gifted people's lives apart from Polly's?

"Well, I dare say he was thought gifted," she said. " I begin to think I did not know him very well."

Her almost throw-away remarks confused Brian. He had expected a different response, a different kind of woman. She seemed strangely detached.

"Well, he was making a name for himself in the College." Brian offered, clutching to the remnants of what he thought he would say.

"I am sure he was," she replied briskly, to Brian's growing discomfort.

"The College needed people like him," Brian persisted. "The old place needed shaking up."

"Oh, he'd do that all right. Will you have some tea?"

She led him into a light and elegant living room where tea was set out on a low table and served in tea-cups. How long since he had drunk tea from a tea-cup? He sat down admiring the room and the view out to the wintry garden. There were lush chairs and cushions and the place was spotless. He compared it with his own home, full of papers and books and pictures. Here there were few signs of daily life or indeed of personality. There were two very large painted vases beside the fireplace and one or two elegant vases on the tables and a stack of silver-framed photographs on the grand piano.

"Who plays the piano?"

"Myself and the girls," she smiled.

"You have two daughters, yes?" Brian had briefed himself from the Vice- Chancellor's secretary.

"That's right. They are away at school"

"It is a lovely home."

"I intend to sell it."

How should he respond? He settled on continuing to make sympathetic remarks about the impact of Tom's death.

"I suppose it would be hard to stay in the house without Tom?"

"You could say that, I suppose, but actually I prefer living in the north. That is where my daughters are at school. Do you have a wife and children, Mr Creed?"

"A wife who is a painter and lectures at the College and a son and daughter. Both children have left home now of course."

"I expect they are clever children with two such clever parents" she said crisply. Brian was embarrassed. When tea was over, he rose to fetch Tom's possessions from the car. The conversation had been getting more and more perplexing. With the piles of things gathered inside the doorway, he asked where it was all to go.

"In my husband's study," she replied. "Then it can all be dealt with at once."

As she led him into a large airy room at the back of the house, she paused. "I have only been in here once since he died, you know, just to dump a few things from his London flat. You probably think that is strange." He knew from his students' behaviour that words spoken in the doorway on the way out were usually important but he couldn't tell whether her reluctance to enter was down to grief or lack of interest. He made no comment.

"Can I leave you to put the stuff in here? If you find

things that ought to go back to the College please take them. I will leave you herc to get on with it."

She left and he looked around. It was very tidy. There was a state-of-the-art computer on the large executive-style mahogany desk. There were no signs of recent work. Brian's desk was chaos by comparison. There were financial books on the shelves and a photograph of his daughters, similar to the one on the piano in the living room, and a framed photograph of him outside the Houses of Parliament with Gordon Brown, no less, and another with Jeremy Paxman, both signed.

Propped against the desk, he suddenly noticed a small painting of Polly's. He sat down suddenly in Tom's chair and looked at in surprise. Did Polly know he had one of her paintings? She had not mentioned it. He then remembered that she told him she had rebuffed him when he first arrived because he was always asking her about paintings about which he was thoroughly ignorant. There were no other paintings in the room and he had noticed only a few prints in the living room. He must tell Polly when they next spoke.

"You'll never guess what," he would say. "I saw one of your paintings in Tom Frost's study at home." She'd be impressed that he had been there. He distributed Tom's books upon the shelves, hung the mackintosh on the back of the door, placed the boxes of papers carefully beside the desk and left feeling very glad to be out of such a soulless room. He returned to the living room.

"Did you find anything you should take back with you?"

"I only recognised a painting of my wife's," he replied, "and I would not dream of removing that."

"Oh, that must have been in his London flat. I cleared that and just dumped the contents in the study."

"My wife had said that he was interested in learning about paintings".

"That is another thing I didn't know about him," she replied.

*   *   *

Veronica arrived for the sitting and asked Polly if she were still prepared to paint her or would she drive back to London before it spread this far west. Polly explained that she was to stay, that she would help Ethel and had already helped Jonty to set up the computer to receive farmers' briefings on the foot and mouth outbreak.

"It's beginning to take over our lives, I fear," said Veronica and in her turn explained that she too would stay and had already moved from Carlisle, in the short-term, into Robert's house to prepare it for selling. "Strange isn't it. Two outsiders, or 'off-comers' as they call us here, making use of the crisis for our own ends."

Polly had prepared the canvas and seated Veronica in the oak chair beside the rug.

"Please go on talking, if you wish. I don't need you to be totally still."

Veronica was more than ready to talk and Polly used the conversation to study her subject.

"I am glad to come back to live where he lived and where we met. Did I tell you he married someone else and they lived in the house after his parents died? I spent happy days in and out of that house in the wild days before the war. I had persuaded my father to buy me a bright red sports car. He was an indulgent father! I used to drive fast through the village and out to the moor up and down steep hills and round long bends and sharp corners, hoping to be admired by Robert as I passed by."

"And was he impressed?"

"He was a very upright person. I was the daring one. I took no thought for the privilege of my situation and none for the poverty around me. I was insufferable!"

Polly was beginning to find that young woman in her lined face.

" I have been thinking about this again since I found some snapshots he took at the time with his box camera. Though he disapproved of me, I thought, I was in nearly every photograph he took. It has felt these few days, browsing among his belongings, that I am falling in love with him all over again and he with me. "

There was a long pause and her face become sad. "These times were to end. I was left to spend a lonely war in the West Cumbrian countryside while he went off to the war. So I moved to Carlisle. And he returned with a wife. It has always had two moods for me, this place – blue skies and shining water or grey skies and gloomy mountains.

"I shall try to capture one of those moods."

Polly put down her brush and they made another date in a week's time.

Veronica stood up stiffly. "Now with this foot and mouth outbreak," she said, "the greyness returns."

Chapter Five

BBC local Radio 4 news
164 cases have been confirmed in Cumbria and 40,000 carcasses are rotting in the fields awaiting disposal'.

Sunday, March 11th, 2001

In the second week of March in South East London on a dull Sunday morning, Brian went into the garden. It was walled in with grey brick and reached by three crumbling steps down from a patio he had built years ago. There were no daffodils yet in flower but there were a few snowdrops in the far corner underneath the plane tree. He picked a small bunch in a fit of nostalgia and put them on the kitchen window-sill in an old paste pot left over from childhood days. The large wooden kitchen table took up most of the space left by the appliances they had accumulated over the years. Polly used to brighten it up for special meals with candles and a cloth.

Jessica and Miles were coming to lunch. Once upon a time they used to eat a proper Sunday lunch. Sundays had a warm and pleasant feel – a last-ditch party before the week - even after Miles and Jessica reached the age to be excused from the ritual. Then Brian and Polly had taken turns to cook, or had gone out for lunch to their favourite pub in Greenwich, or, until a year ago, had invited friends and colleagues or favoured students. They'd thus brought life into Sundays even in winter. When Miles left home to set up on his own in North London, Brian had turned his bedroom into a study, installing a new desk for his computer, leaving Miles's bed blocking the window in a half expectation that he might one day return. When Jessica moved out Polly had similarly moved her computer and papers into Jessica's room leaving the bed and wall coverings as they were. But she had spent little time there.

That was when he began to dread Sundays. He would go upstairs to work after breakfast and she would go to her College studio. The lunch parties stopped. There had never seemed a good enough reason to stop working. This pattern had been going on for at least eighteen months. Last winter had been dark and unrewarding and he'd generally slept on Sunday afternoons. This year he'd been alone every Sunday since Polly drove off on her mission. One Sunday only had been memorable when a trace of snow had given him the energy to walk to Greenwich Park and savour the view, recalling Miles, as a child, kicking a football down the long slope to the Queen's House, causing him to retrieve it while Polly, with the baby that was Jessica, laughed at him from the top of the hill. Other Sundays consisted of a slower than usual start to a day of marking, report writing and doing his washing, with a joyless attempt at cooking his own lunch. All day he was waiting to call Polly. Then, she would ask after his work about which he was non-committal to avoid her lack of interest. She would ask after Miles and Jessica but he had learnt that she was speaking to them more frequently than he was. Because she wanted to be completely undisturbed, she had refused to take her computer up there so he couldn't even e-mail her.

She had told him last Sunday that she had been sketching for a large oil painting of a particular mountain but, for no reason he could understand, had also begun a portrait of some woman she had met, "until the situation clears up." He expressed his pessimism about the duration of the thing from what he had been reading in the 'Guardian'.

"Why don't you come back? You could paint portraits here. The situation is clearly getting out of control."

"Brian, fancy you reading all that foot and mouth stuff?"

"Aren't you?"

She confessed that she didn't read the papers though she heard the local news.

"You're not even interested are you?" he said in a scathing tone.

Even without this unfortunate epidemic, he found the time and the place of her trip increasingly odd. Did she not realise that the weather on the North West coast would be bad in February and

March? In spite of the adverse conditions she had now landed herself in, she was continuing to do just what she wanted. As he moved about the kitchen he was aware of the continuous undercurrent of negativity in his monologues about her. He slammed down the saucepan of potatoes and parsnips. She clearly now thought nothing of him or their marriage.

However, this Sunday would be like old times - lunch in the old style. He'd tried to remember what they used to eat and had even found a recipe for a chocolate pudding that seemed easy to cook. He was almost enjoying himself. The doorbell would soon be ringing so he put on some cheerful Handel and chose a good Rioja. He lit the fire in the living room and set the kitchen table with the best glasses and a red linen cloth that he found in the airing cupboard adding dark green paper napkins left over from Christmas.   He even found a candle to place in the middle of the table.

Then they arrived together, these grown up children of his. They'd brought him presents too. Jessica rushed around the house calling out that he was keeping it clean and tidy, which he did, apart from his study, and then they all three sat down around the fire to drink a beer. Why had he not done this before?

Lunch went surprisingly well. That is until Jessica skittishly began to question Miles about her suspicions that he had a girlfriend. Miles stalled but this did not daunt her, despite Brian's attempt at restraint.

"But Dad," she burst out, "he must be having it off with someone he shouldn't or he'd tell us."

"It is not our business," said Brian quietly.

"Well, I think it is. I know people who have affairs with other people's partners and it is not on!"

"Maybe you do, we all may, but it is still not our business," persisted Brian. "Why are you getting so upset about it? I don't understand."

Miles at last rose to the bait. "It's because you can't find anyone of your own, I expect. You're constructing this fairy story about me out of pure jealousy. What about your Frenchman?

What's happened to him?"

"Don't you mention that," spat Jessica and before Brian could stop them they were pitching into conflict as if they were teenagers again with the result that Miles became very flushed and eventually stood up angrily.

"If you must know, I am in love with a wonderful person and, yes, actually she is married."

"I knew it!" crowed Jessica.

There was a shocked silence broken by Brian.

" I think you should say sorry to Miles. He did not mean to tell us this and we should now respect the fact that he wanted to keep it private."

Jessica pouted, "I am not sorry. He should be honest."

Miles sat down in a mixture of defiance and distress.

"Well, now you know if that pleases you. And to *be honest* I am proud of it. It is wonderful even though it is also terrible. You've no idea what it is like. You've no right to stand in judgment. What do you know about anything? I might have told you in time but dragging it out of me is all wrong."

"We agree then! I too think it is all very wrong!" retorted Jessica,

"Have you got some sort of born-again religion or what?" Miles stood up angrily, wedging his chair between the table and the windowsill "This bloody table!"

"Oh so it's the table's fault, is it?" shouted Jessica. "So this married woman then - she's got children, has she?"

Miles pushed his way out of the constricted space, dragging the tablecloth with him and crashing plates onto the floor.

"Dad, I'll go now. It was a lovely lunch and I appreciate the thought, but I refuse to talk about anything while she is here with her mean, spinsterly, fundamentalist views!"

As Brian followed him sadly to the door, Miles turned to him to say, "You'll tell Mum tonight I expect."

'It is up to you whether you tell her, Miles, it is not up to me."

"Thanks Dad." And Brian gave him the first hug he had

given him for a long time.

Miles's departure was greeted by a sobbing Jessica, flinging herself into the arm-chair. When she could speak, she was full of remorse but only at how she had spoiled the occasion.

"It is as if the evil spirit of old Sunday lunches had come back to haunt us," she said and appealed to Brian for agreement that Miles was being stupid.

"Jessica, I simply do not understand why you are so angry."

Jessica cried harder and he tried to comfort her as he had done Miles, but she pushed him away. She remarked bitterly that if her mother had been here, a very different discussion would have taken place.

"She is not a liberal wimp like you!" She flounced out slamming the door behind her.

Brian was left to clear up the remains of the meal alone in dismay - a mood he tried to drown with a glass of brandy.

" So much for trying!"

Jessica on the other hand, walked fiercely up the hill and around the empty Sunday streets for half an hour before going back to her room. She put on her loudest music and flung around the items of rejected clothing she had left in heaps on her bed until a loud banging from the Oaf brought her out on to the landing to give vent to loud shouts of protest at his intrusion into her privacy.

*   *   *

Polly had not been truthful about her level of interest in the epidemic. It was impossible not to be drawn into the developing drama. Even though the outbreaks were in the north east of the county, with the footpaths closed around all the Cumbrian fells the village was living through a siege, awaiting the invasion of the virus. The place had always seemed quiet to her, but it was now eerily so. The milk lorries still rumbled in and out but had assumed a sinister character crossing the boundaries of the empty village as a reminder of the threat outside. The bus to and from town still came and went but Ethel had told her that everything else was cancelled – evening classes, Mothers' Union, the W.I.

"Most of us are farmers' wives," Ethel had explained to her on the phone.

Polly learnt that the regular village hall events and even the Hunt Ball -" just a glorified hop in the village hall really," Ethel had said - were not to take place this year. There were no cars parked outside the pub or the village hall and, though the church bell rang briefly on Sunday morning, '*to remind us of the prayers offered to those directly affected*', Polly had read in the parish magazine, she saw few people going in.

She had pictured herself traversing the countryside, sketching and painting, and discovering a way of grieving that would put the past at rest and clarify her future. She looked to be restored by the natural beauty around her. Yet now, it was as if a storm-cloud hung over the fields, over the fells, down the lanes. Spring was coming and birds were singing and she had seen violets in the hedgerow but instead of bringing delight, these signs were a poignant contrast to the suffering filmed every night on the television. Far from assuaging her own grief, the atmosphere was pressing her further into it. It was immobilising her. After the first violent outbursts and dreadful dreams, she was again stuck. The image of Tom was fading and she had to force herself to remember details of his appearance. She found herself sitting in the barn in the evenings, not dozing, but as if in hibernation. She would rouse herself to find that an hour or more had passed and she had no recollection of how.

And she was acutely aware that her neighbours were also trapped. For them this was a disaster, a plague, waiting to reach them. Ethel telephoned her frequently on one pretext or another and Polly realised that this woman previously of few words, now needed to talk. On this Sunday afternoon at about five o'clock, she again telephoned.

"I'm sorry to trouble you on a Sunday," she began "but

Sunday can be a long day and I'm just making sure you're all right."

Then, lapsing into tears she said that all of Jim's brother's sheep and his herd of cows had been diagnosed with the disease and had been destroyed.

"Just imagine, Mrs Creed, the whole lot, all that they had been keeping for thirty years. Thirty years' work in that place, they've had. All gone! Just came and served the order and then took them."

"What happened next?" Polly asked.

"Shot. They came and herded them into groups, in pens or in the yard, and shot them. Annie said they could hear it all. Then they are just left lying around in heaps. Terrible smell, Mrs Creed. Terrible! The sheep waiting to be burnt and the cows to be buried. There are great burial sites and huge pyres all over the countryside but they have to wait their turn!"

"I saw it on the television." Polly said. The powerful image had indeed stayed in her mind.

"Well that was right near their farm. Might have been their stock you saw."

"How dreadful for them."

"Well, I don't mind telling you, Mrs Creed, our Annie was crying and crying over the phone. She said some of the wives had been going out and throwing flowers on the fire, can you believe, but Annie said she wouldn't go near the place when their turn came. She went on to say that the terrible thing everywhere was the silence. No sound of animals shifting about in their stalls. No more sound of the milking machine."

"Of course."

"And they are worrying that the fumes might be dangerous with all that old wood and stuff." Then she added in a conspiratorial tone, "Jim says the government had it all planned beforehand"

"Surely not," said Polly, the disbelief of the city dweller sounding in her voice.

"Well, Mrs Creed, the government has been stocking up

railway sleepers for the purpose since last year, so Jim says."

"But, they can't have known," began Polly.

"You just don't know. Nobody but us up here knows. The government don't want us to keep so many animals, that is what it boils down to…rather get their supermarket meat and milk from France or Holland or China or Timbuctoo! Cheap food! That is what this is all about. You city folk have no idea what is going on."

"Your husband doesn't think it will come here, does he?"

"That's just it, you see, you can't tell any more on account of all the stock that's been travelling so far these days, you know, to different markets. We're made to be price-mad nowadays, never mind what suits the animals and the farmer, so the virus can have been carried all over and it's hard to track and impossible to prevent. We're just…. " She stopped halfway through her explanation. "Listen to me going on at you like this. You're up here for a quiet time and there's me going on."

"It is so terrible for you all."

"You're right there but I shouldn't be troubling you. I talk to Annie my sister-in-law and other wives all the time. There is even a Helpline for us to talk to. Everyone is feeling so cut off and grim these days. I fear for Jim and Jonty, I really do. And that reminds me. We're so grateful to you for getting the computer going again. Jonty is on it all the time. They can't go to the markets to pick up local news, you see. So it is good luck that you were here."

"Is the computer the main way of knowing what is going on?"

"Oh yes, it's big now. They send us messages through all the time. It's not only the government site Jonty looks at but some other that's better. The Ministry's a mess, Mrs Creed, I can tell you, a big mess. They can't get anything right!"

Polly was warming to Ethel day by day. She was strong and passionate about her family and animals, in fact her whole way of life. Animals meant much more to her than Polly could ever have realised and she was daily humbled by her city ignorance. There was also a faithfulness about the way Ethel conducted herself that was in marked contrast to her own life. She, it now seemed to her, had become dangerously uprooted from the loyalties that Ethel took as her mainstay.

It was Sunday night and her turn to telephone Brian. How could she explain to him, even to herself, that she was going to stay despite the epidemic? She felt useful but she also knew that in truth she dreaded to return. She was, in effect, putting Tom and herself way ahead of any loyalty to Brian and had long been doing so. She knew that her consequent coolness to Brian hurt and perplexed him and had contributed to his growing bitterness and the depression she could hear in his voice. Brian had once been her bedrock. She now mused on the word "bedrock" with its bracketed contrast of image and texture. She looked up the word in a dictionary she found on the shelves - it was the hard rock beneath gravel or loose surface soil. Her life, since the children had left home, seemed to consist entirely of loose surface soil. When she met Brian, he was a successful teacher. She had admired his confidence and the way he related to his pupils and colleagues with humour and kindliness. He acted in the role of mentor long before such a role had been fashionably invented. He had fitted her image of a Welsh rugby player – dark curly hair, a swarthy complexion, a high colour and strong shoulders. His parents were Welsh Baptists and her more liberal parents had warned her that he might not appreciate her feminist views. But instead of mocking them he had affirmed them. He asked her to marry him within a week of their first date. He was, even then, a man of principle and his parents' principles they largely were. What would he think if he knew how she had deceived him. She found herself wishing for Ethel's simplicity.

Old Welsh gloom seemed, partly because of her perhaps, to be emerging in Brian's very soul. He was always expecting the worst and was angry about any authority imposed on him. He was critical of the Vice-Chancellor and the professors in his school, with a perpetual chip on his shoulder. She had become worn down by his complaints. When she saw two sides of a question, he saw this as a challenge to himself. He claimed that she didn't understand him and was so easily hurt by her comments that she became permanently on her guard. He then called her cold. He also bundled together under the title of 'cold', her encouragement to the independence of Miles and Jessica, leaving them to work out their own problems. She tried always to plan their own lives to avoid conflict but he did not like 'planning', saying it smacked of work. He had struggled to control his resentment when she was offered her new job and from that moment, they seemed only to talk in order to check their diaries. Bit by bit, their sex-life became just as perfunctory.

Before meeting Tom she had dealt with this by focussing on her work, rushing from one thing to another, head down, like a dog following a scent. She had an exciting job and adored visiting the major galleries, building their latest exhibitions into her courses, linking her students with the new artists breaking into the London art scene. She had become almost reckless in her pursuit of opportunities and ideas. She slept little and ate little. She would have gone on in this way had Tom not pulled her off course. Tom had acknowledged his mid-life crisis from the start but she had never considered hers. She now saw that she had been draining herself dry. Driven by ambition, trying at the same time to avoid upstaging Brian, flattered by the praise she received from colleagues and students and stimulated by contacts with prestigious galleries, she had been intoxicated by success. She was proud of what she had done and could do. But at the same time she had become inwardly depleted. She had come to feel as hard and polished as a stone.

And then she had fallen in love. As if by some ancient alchemy stone turned to liquid gold. She could see it all as a surreal painting. She became more secretive than a teenager, seizing the love of a virtual stranger and allowing him to become closer to her than she had ever allowed anyone else to be.

She could suddenly no longer summon up Tom's face and rushed upstairs to check on the portrait by her bed. She was sitting on the bed looking at it when the telephone rang. She ran downstairs clutching the sketch. It was Miles on the phone.

"What's it like up there Mum? Are you all right?"

"Yes of course I am, though it is like a siege."

Polly began to explain the restrictions, the precautions and the horror for the farmers and their families, destroying their way of life and their livelihoods. Miles was taken aback by the strength of her reaction.

"It sounds awful. Why not come back while you can? If you're working in abstract, you don't need to be there do you?"

"Darling?" Polly was surprised by Miles' attempt at understanding her work. "You know about abstracts do you?"

"Well, someone said something like that."

"So, who exactly were you talking to about my work?"

"Oh… a friend… well actually, mother. A good friend."

Polly waited.

"I think I'm in love."

"Ah."

"And I've had a row with Jess about her."

"With Jess? Why ever with Jess?"

Miles described Brian's Sunday lunch and how Jessica had chosen the occasion to force him to tell them about his girlfriend. Polly recalled the laughing young woman she had seen outside the restaurant.

"And then Jess just went berserk; absolutely lost it!"

"Why, Miles?"

"Because she's married, that's why."

There was a silence.

"I saw her, didn't I?" she said.

"Yes, Mum, you did"

"She looked lovely."

"She is." Miles took a deep breath. "but she has a husband and a child."

Polly glanced down at the portrait in her hand.

"Say something, Mum, or I shall think you disapprove like Jess. She was vitriolic. I tell you, Mum. I was shocked by her." More silence. "Mum. Are you shocked by me?"

"No, of course not." She gathered herself together. "But what does it mean to you, Miles?"

"I guess it means happiness and, well, pain". In a small voice and after another long silence, Polly said, "Thanks for telling me Miles."

"Thanks for not jumping down my throat. Dad was decent too," he added.

"And she? Is it hard for her?"

"Oh yes. She is in London during the week and has to go home to Leeds on Fridays to be with them."

"So, she's living a double life."

"Oh yes, it's much, much harder for her."

Another pause while Polly struggled between empathy for her son and the paralysis of her own situation.

"Couldn't you meet her, even talk with her?" Miles urged. "She's not like the others. Mum… I know it's asking a lot, but can't you come home? Especially now that this thing has broken out where you are. Maybe you *should* come home."

Looking at Tom's picture, she said. "This 'thing' as you call it means that if I came I wouldn't come back here again".

"Would that matter?"

"Yes, Miles, it would rather."

"Why Mum?" Miles would not let go yet.

"Well I came here to work," Polly stated flatly.

Miles must, at that point, have decided to ask his awkward question. Polly was waiting for it.

"You know that day you saw me," he ventured. "Who were *you* with?"

"Just a colleague." Polly knew she sounded on her guard.

"Dare I say that it looked a bit more than that?"

"Well," she quipped, "he was a very friendly sort of man."

"Was?"

"Well….he's not around any more."

"That's not why you didn't say anything about me?"

"What's her name?" Polly abruptly changed the subject.

"Sue. And I couldn't bear it if she left me." Silence. "So

you can't be much help to me at the moment."

"That sounds terrible."

"Can you tell Dad and Jess that I've told you? Jess is sure to ring you."

"Of course. Goodnight Miles……. and good luck with it. We'll talk again."

She put down the phone and sat in the chair exhausted. The collusion she and Miles had entered in Soho had become cross-screwed. She had failed him.

*   *   *

She was roused by the phone call from Brian. He immediately pitched into an account of his doomed Sunday lunch. She said she had heard about it from Miles. Had he told her about the married girlfriend? Yes, she said, her name is Sue. Brian seemed to see it as a growing up experience for Miles… one he would get over. He was more worried about Jessica who had behaved cruelly, he said, forcing a confession out of Miles and then rushing off in a temper.

"They're missing you, I think," he said tentatively, "but you're staying all the same, I gather."

"I have simply not been able to do enough work yet." Here she was again. Blocking, blocking, using work as a shield.

"Well, you'll do what you want to do, I know that only too well" he said coldly, "though I must say, if it were me, I'd be back before things there get worse. Pretty grim if you ask me".

"It isn't that bad just here," she lied.

"Oh, by the way" he changed the subject "you'll never guess what. I visited Marjorie Frost this week. You know, Tom Frost's widow – at the request of the VC as a matter of fact - and there in his study – I was taking back some of the things from his office - I found one of your paintings. You know one of the ones you put into the last exhibition?"

"I know the one, Brian."

"You never told me he bought it."

"Didn't I?"

"Well, he'd had it in his London flat apparently. Funny coincidence, I thought".

"No big deal," she replied. "He'd more money than sense perhaps."

By the time she went to bed she has been assailed by a further burst of the old familiar anxiety. Marjorie Frost had gone to the flat and found her painting there. She had never looked at the walls. She had totally forgotten the painting above the bed. Should she have brought it away with her? No, that would have created more problems than it solved. Now, because of the painting, Marjorie Frost might suspect, as Brian might, that, however remote it might seem, there was a connection between herself and Tom.

The rain and wind were beating on the roof light above her bed. She began to panic again that the affair would come to light. She recalled a phrase used at the inquest by the woman in the car: 'By a hair's breadth.'

*   *   *

The following morning, she switched on the local radio to hear that there were at last cases in Cumbria. After breakfast, she drove the four miles into town with the image of dead carcasses in her mind's eye. Compared with earlier trips, the town was deserted. The shop lights were lit but there were few people in the streets. The bakery was nearly out of bread; everyone else must have come early and scurried home again. Some of the remnants of the Christmas decorations were still hanging down the centre of the High Street, damp and twirling. When bustling with life, there was nothing grim about the town's grey stone buildings, the surrounds of their rectangular windows painted green or blue or brown. What was the elusive word she'd seen in a title in the bookshop? Cumbria's 'vernacular style?' But now the town had lost its purpose. It could be any town under siege. The people hurrying through the streets with scarves and hoods against the wind were not looking for conversation. No cheerful shouting across the road today. In one shop, unsure what brand to buy, she mentioned Ethel's name and the right stuff was produced and a quick interest expressed in how Ethel was bearing up. The woman serving her had heard about Jim's brother in Longtown losing his flocks and herds.

"She's as well as can be expected. I'm doing some shopping for her," she explained as if Ethel were ill.

"That's very good of you. Are you a visitor then?"

Polly nodded.

"Well, that's good then. We could do with more of you but they'll not be here this year. The town will suffer as well as the farmers."

She drove home, determined to get on with her work to justify her stay. She must get things in proportion. She was being thanked for being here as if she were doing them a favour!

∗　　　　　　∗　　　　　　∗

Brian thought about the business of not sleeping as he went upstairs to bed. Most nights and early mornings he thought about not sleeping. Since Polly drove off, his night-time patterns had totally changed. He would fall asleep over the ten o'clock news and then wake in the early hours of the morning feeling alone in the bed. Despondency thrived in the early hours when he believed his career and marriage were both over.

He would lie awake, retracing his life from schoolboy promise to middle-aged decline. Both his grandfathers were miners in neighbouring Welsh villages and neither grandmother had ever worked. Poverty was their expectation and their experience. But Brian's father escaped the mines and moved the family to Cardiff where Brian worked hard to please them; they were almost in awe of his success and were certainly in awe of Polly when he took her to meet them. She had grown up in Surrey with ambitious, prosperous parents and was not only clever but beautiful. His parents concealed their views about mothers working when they should be looking after their children. Now they were both dead and if he were to be made redundant or were his marriage to fail, thankfully they would never know.

He retraced the story of their marriage. Polly had been the student teacher catch of the year and it was he who had caught her. They married quickly, in part, to reassure his parents who would have been shocked if they had lived together without a wedding whereas Polly's parents feigned open-mindedness. Polly was doubly committed - to her children and to her career - which he admired - but he had come to resent the way she ran the family as she ran her job, thinking of every eventuality and plastering the house with time-tables. He would rather just come home to the kitchen table and talk. Recently the feverishness of her work and her constant absences had got to him. When conflict occurred over a diary clash she would try to organise it away and he would give in with ill humour. This was the pattern in their marriage. They didn't row. Once a dispute had reached a point when it would be de-stabilising to go further, they would utter their standard rebukes.

"Why can't you ever say what you really feel! You are so morose."

"You simply don't have any feelings any more. You are so cold."

The habit spread to sex too. He never asked her for sex, fearing that she would turn away, and she never asked him, believing, he could only suppose, that it was his job to initiate it. And they never discussed this. Not once. They continued to make love only on Sunday mornings and lately not then. Now he badly wanted her back.

As dawn crept into the sky, he resolved that when, if, she returned, he would do what she accused him of never doing: he would say what he felt. He would tell her that he loved her and needed her. He then switched on Radio 4 only to find himself listening to the early farming news, when the deadly statistics and whereabouts of foot and mouth would be intoned, followed by interviews with distraught, angry and cynical farmers. If she was under siege, he felt himself no less so.

The following morning he had an urgent message to see the Vice-Chancellor at the close of day. The man had been in post for two and a half years. As for many vice-chancellors, his staff had concluded that, though an academic, he had discovered a talent for, and preferred the life-style of, a corporate chief executive. At the time of his appointment, it was the College view that he had applied for the job because his chances of getting a chair were zero. He was bound therefore to be a new broom to prove himself to himself as much as to the rest of them. He was certainly energetic, determinedly good at personal contacts and terrier-like at sniffing out fundraising opportunities. His son had set up a 'dot.com business' apparently. His emphasis on finance, private enterprise and economics was therefore unsurprising. No point in staff protests as he was unswervingly dedicated to radical change and 'the bottom line'. Brian and his 'purist' colleagues, as he thought of them, became resigned to their views being swept aside at Council meetings and Faculty Boards.

Brian had taken this gloomy view when the Vice-Chancellor announced the expansion of the Business School to be led by the media economist and finance and business pundit, Tom Frost.

"I expect he's got the Midas touch," he had remarked to his neighbour in the Council meeting.

"He's a catch all right," replied his colleague, "or he'd better be. They say it takes a million to endow a chair and another million for the poor bugger to make it work. He must have attracted that somehow."

"Trouble with us is there's no money in it," commented Brian.

He turned his attention back to Tom's C.V. being read out by the Vice-Chancellor.

"What have I been doing all my life?" snarled his neighbour.

"It's all part of this New Labour stuff. Education and

Social Policy only get a mention when the far left rears its head. This lot is the new adrenalin!" Brian was rather pleased with this phrase. "Like all these dot-coms everyone talks about."

And then, to his surprise, he had got to like the man. He had charm. That alone did not endear him but Brian came to view him favourably because of his support for education. He talked to Brian passionately about its importance as the moral centre of the place and had taken to asking detailed questions about Brian's department, making him feel that he, Tom, would be on his side when he needed him. He watched out for him on late night television news programmes, shouting to Polly to watch, although she was always on her way to bed those nights when she was home early. He was a man at ease in the modern world. Yet, he had been impressed by the apparent congruity between the man on the screen and the man with whom he occasionally had lunch.

"What's he doing wasting his time with us?"

"What indeed. Makes you wonder," said a colleague.

But Tom's death, at a stroke, had seemed to make his own position more vulnerable.

"Pity we haven't got Tom to take them on," he remarked.

"He'd have got out by now if he'd had any sense."

"Well, he got out all right." The rejoinder hung uneasily in the air.

*   *   *

The Vice-Chancellor's private office, that he had never before entered, was extremely tidy with a bigger managerial desk and a larger carpet than anyone else's. His P.A. was slipping out brightly as Brian arrived.

"Goodnight Michael, Goodnight Brian," she called.

He was glad to be on first name terms.   The Vice-Chancellor motioned him to sit down across the desk, swept the papers from it into his left-hand drawer and pushed back his chair. Brian recalled the muddle he had left on his own desk and the state of his overflowing drawers. 'A clear desk policy,' was a phrase he'd heard spoken around.

"Brian. Thanks for coming," the VC began. "I have a tricky matter to share with you and asked you at the end of the day so that we would not be disturbed." Brian waited.

"First, how did you find Marjorie Frost?"

"Well, all right I guess."

"Poor woman. Terrible way to lose someone," said the V.C shaking his head. Brian nodded. "Did she seem very upset?"

Brian did not know how to respond to this. "She seems a very reserved person".

"Ah yes. Reserved". There was a silence as he twiddled his pen.

"Well, I'm asking you to explore matters a bit further with her," the VC continued to twiddle his pen and to rescue it by banging it on the desk when it slipped from his fingers.

"As a matter of fact I am in a real difficulty. You see, our own financial guru - you know Terry, good man. Well, he's found some odd things. Before I go on, Brian, I must ask if you would be prepared to keep to yourself what I am going to say."

"Can you tell me why me?" Brian managed to ask.

"Of course, you have a right not to listen to any more, but I have come to you because you have already met his wife, widow, rather, and you are not likely to go about making capital out of anything I say. You're a discreet kind of man, I believe, with a good moral sense. I respect that."

"Thank you."

"So you will keep this to yourself?" Brian nodded. "Well, it appears that there are some holes in the Business Studies Department's accounts."

"Holes?"

"Yes, quite big holes, in fact. You know, money that should be there is not where it should be."

Tom thought of Polly's comment "more money than sense". "Go on" he said.

"Well it appears likely that some of it has been used outside the university accounting system."

"By whom?

"Well, by him personally, paying for things not accounted for – we don't know how or what yet and we've no way of finding out easily. Any of his pre-College stuff that he might have kept in his office, went with you to his home before we learnt of the hole and there is nothing in his College files to explain the gaps."

"How much is missing?"

"More than half a million." It seemed to hurt the VC to even think of it let alone say it. "Much more, actually."

"Could there be an innocent explanation?"

"That is what I want to find out before I call in the auditors."

"And you think I can ask Mrs Frost?"

"Not directly of course. Not fair to her at all. But I thought you might begin gently, you know, start small and quiet, and perhaps find out, for example, who his solicitor might be or his previous finance company contacts we might sound out, informally of course, about the kind of projects with which Tom might have been involved."

Brian began to imagine how difficult he would find it to bring the topic up.

"It won't be easy," he said.

"No, of course not, but I think you can do it if anyone can."

"You won't want me to press too far, I take it."

"No, no. You're not being asked to investigate. We'd have to do that later if indicated but you might give us a lead to the best people to approach."

Brian was alarmed. "You are not suggesting I tell her of your concerns."

"Oh Lord no."

"Who else knows about this?"

"Just myself and Terry at the moment."

"I see."

"You'll do it?"

"What do you want me to ask?"

"Ask her in general terms what she knew of the scope of the work that he might have continued outside the College and whether she has been drawn into any discussions about it with anyone since he died or whether he confided in anyone in particular that she knew about. He must have been a wealthy man, you know, up with all the latest developments. Hang it, that's why we wanted him - to bring us up to the minute and recruit bright students and research money with a sound financial outcome. Hmmm. Perhaps she knew of projects with which he was involved that might throw light on any activities of which we were not aware at the time of his death."

"Sounds a bit vague."

"Yes, I'm afraid it does, yes."

"She did say she wondered if she really knew him."

"Did she indeed," said the VC looking concerned. He went on to explain that he was the kind of man who must have made a range of investments. As he was using his contacts to build up his department, he may already have made unrecorded contracts, you know, offers to individuals to join him that might have legal implications for the College now for example. That sort of thing. You get the picture? What was the overlap, you see." Brian did not see and was not sure the VC did either. But of course they would not want Brian to mention concrete matters like that. "Just feel around perhaps. She might know how he operated." They did not want to go to any of his financial contacts at this point if they could find out more from, "shall we say, a confidential source?"

"I see," said Brian very uncertainly. "Wouldn't someone with more financial acumen perform this sort of task better?"

"I've thought about that but they would be tempted to investigate and that would not be fair on his widow, would it. It might frighten her off, you see, and yet she might give you a lead that would avoid any unpleasantness and be a way of keeping in touch with her in case we need to pursue things with her any further."

"And I wouldn't frighten her." Good old Brian again!

"Exactly so. Well, do what you can, eh? There's a good chap. At the very least get the name of her solicitor."

Brian walked away with his head in a spin. What had Tom been up to? Perhaps this clever man was not as clever as he'd thought. He wondered again why he had come to the College if he was such a financial wizard. He had not been frank with the V.C. about his impression of Marjorie. She was oddly detached and bitter. She seemed to want to wash her hands of her husband. Perhaps grief did strange things to people.

*   *   *

As soon as she woke the day after the Sunday lunch debacle, Jessica knew she had behaved badly. Why did she always realise things too late? She had been trying to trap Miles into confessing that he was having an affair with an unavailable woman but it turned out to be a cruel act especially in front of her father. She had spoiled his attempt to re-create a family occasion without Polly. She turned over in bed in misery. She was a fool! She'd have to make it up to them. She wouldn't tell her Mum as that is just what Miles would think she would do. She wouldn't go and cry on her Dad either. The mature thing would be to go and see Miles and say she was sorry. She'd go this evening after College.

She sat through a boring tutorial concealing her lack of work and had lunch with a few mates who remarked that she was glum. Of course she told them why and then thought afterwards that she shouldn't be so blabby. Their response to Miles's affair was "So what?" "Everyone's does it." "No big deal." For her, it was a big deal. She intended to be totally loyal to anyone she had a relationship with – if she ever had one that is. You shouldn't cheat on a partner nor poach someone else's. People always got hurt that way as she had always said.

As the Oaf was out when she returned home, she had a shower and dressed as non-sexually as she could to discourage any rapists around on the underground and set off to apologise. She got to Miles's pad at seven o'clock in the evening and rang the bell. To her astonishment the door was opened by this blond person, with long hair.

"Hi there!"

"Hullo," said Jessica gruffly.

"I'm Sue," said the blond person, "You must be Jessica. Miles said you'd probably turn up. He's been ringing you."
Jessica had not anticipated that this person would be so brazenly there.

"Do come in and don't look so shocked," said Sue brightly. "I'll leave you two alone shall I? He's in the kitchen."
Jessica stumbled in through the door and made her way into the kitchen. There stood Miles cooking something pretty amazing by the smell. He had on a butcher's apron and was wielding a fish slice over a large flat frying pan in which he was flavouring a smart looking oil with several cloves of garlic and some grey-green herbs. She was impressed.

"Hi Sis! Come to apologise?"

"I don't see why I should," she bridled, not saying what she intended to say at all.

"Well, you were well out of order, forcing me to tell Dad about Sue. I was going to tell him and Mum in my own good time."

"So you think it's all right do you, going out with a married woman?

"No, of course I don't think it's all right. It's hellish and I thought you might have grasped that last night. But life isn't always as smooth as ice-cream." He added some strips of fish to the pan and swirled them around. "Will you want some of this when I have finished it?"

"It is hellish for Sue too I suppose," she spat out.

"Dead right it is."

"What are you going to do about it then?"

"Don't know, Sis. No offence but this is not your problem is it?" He tipped in a glass of white wine and then stirred in some very thin cooked spaghetti and swirled that around. "Now are you going to sit down with us like a normal person and eat in a civilised way?"

"I dare say she is OK, she looks OK, but it's wrong Miles and you ought to stop it. "

"I'm twenty six, Jessica. Grown up. Left home. Working it out between us, Sue and I. Not your business. Now are you going to sit down?"

Instead of accepting the olive-branch, she did the opposite and turning away to hide her tears made for the front door and slammed it shut behind her.

Sue came into the kitchen.

"Nearly ready," said Miles. "Are you happy with mullet in white wine?" He behaved as if nothing untoward had taken place.

"I seem to have lost my appetite," she said quietly, adding, after a pause " in more ways than one."

Miles dished out the meal and sat down, only then looking at Sue who was sitting still and straight and unhappy.

"Come on, eat up. You mustn't let my little sister's views affect you. What I do, what we do, has nothing to do with her."

"Doesn't it?"

"For fuck's sake, Sue!" He banged the table in sudden frustration, " I will not have my sister come here and try to come between us. That is just what she wants."

" 'For fuck's sake' is just about right."

"Sue," he groaned, putting his head in his hands. "You simply can't think that is what this is about, what we are about. I love you."

Sue still did not move.

"Sue," he pleaded, "please, please talk to me."

Sue pushed back her chair, got up and walked out of the kitchen.

"I know it's hard for you," he said as she went out, "but we're all right aren't we?"

He sat down again for a moment before following her, expecting that he would find her waiting to sort things out. But then he heard the front door click. She had picked up her overnight bag and gone.

Jessica waited for what seemed ages on the tube station platform, tear-stained and wretched, until an elderly woman asked her if she was feeling ill. How humiliating was that! When she arrived at her station, she half-ran and half-walked up the hill to her room and flung herself onto the bed sobbing, "why does everything I do go so wrong!" until the Oaf banged on the ceiling.

*   *   *

As the week passed, Polly got more phone calls from Ethel. A short phone call would become a long one. She at first thought that Ethel was checking up that she was observing the travel restrictions but it became clear that she simply wanted to talk about her family's plight and the plight of her friends. Like most wives on Cumbrian small family farms, Polly gathered, she was cook and housekeeper and the one to look after the farmyard, feeding the ducks and hens and cats and dogs. But now she was worrying whether the ducks would fly off and carry back the virus and whether the dogs would drink the water left standing on the bio-security at the gate. In a normal winter, she said, they kept the cows in the sheds for calving and she fed the ones that were slow to feed. Now she was worrying that one might have a breach birth because Jim was vowing he'd never let a vet over the threshold, blaming them for spreading the virus.

"And, Mrs Creed, I don't mind saying, the men are getting under my feet!"

She explained that they would normally be out now spreading muck on those fields they kept for cultivation and otherwise mending fences, gates and hedges for when the cows went out in May when the grass was sweet? But she doubted the cows would get out this May?

"How many cows do you have?" Polly asked, embarrassed by her total ignorance.

"Seventy for milking and nineteen for beef. And, with the markets closed, we can't send any to market, including the calves, so they all have to be squeezed into the sheds, with the calves kept apart from their mothers lest they bond. If the epidemic goes on into the Spring, the overcrowding will get even worse and they'll miss the best of the grass which'll bring down the quality of the milk all spring and summer."

"Really," said Polly, imagining the unimaginable.

"So you see, I'm worrying all the time," said Ethel. "I can understand some farmers saying that the ones who lose their cattle will be better off. The only thing we've got to be thankful for is that we didn't take sheep off the fells for wintering this year, as Jonty wanted his dad to do."

Polly thought of her brief trips around the fells and the total disregard she had had for what went on there.

"So now," Ethel continued, "we're all shoved up against each other in the house like the cows in the sheds!' And Jonty and Jim never did get on at the best of times. Father and son, you know."

Before all this had happened, apparently, they would go to the market most weeks buying or selling and keeping an eye on prices. They would come home a bit the worse for drink, Ethel said, and Jim would sleep in his armchair after supper and Jonty would go off to the pub in the village. She would be out herself, to the WI or the Mothers' Union, or the lace-making class. It was her job to supply milk for these gatherings, packing up her basket with tea-cakes covered with a cloth, "just like my mother before me."

"You see, Mrs Creed, we live rather separate social lives, the men and the women. We women get a good crack that way and so do the men. It's always been like that round here."

Polly's views on women's roles and career opportunities belonged to a different world.

"And now there's no kiddies running about the village. Even the Mothering Sunday service is to be cancelled. You need that sort of lift after the winter. The visiting vicar is doing his best to keep things cheerful but there's not much he can do.

Everywhere is so silent." Then she added abruptly. "I hope Jonty hasn't been troubling you at all, Mrs Creed. Just you let me know if he does, won't you and I'll see to it."

*   *   *

Polly had been fearing that her project to paint Veronica would also stop. So she was relieved when she arrived at her door, as arranged. Polly embraced her and took her long coat to hang on the inside of the barn door.

"I thought you wouldn't be able to come!"

"I am rather enjoying this, you know."

"Good," said Polly "though I warn you, you might not enjoy the portrait."

"It's always good to have an off-comer like you in the place. We Cumbrians have a habit of sounding welcoming but privately feeling otherwise."

"Do you still feel part of the village then?" Polly liked Veronica to talk while she worked.

"In some ways, not others. I belong to the past and I think some of the old ones thought Robert should have married me in the first place. When he didn't I was totally shattered, so I think the village felt sorry for me. So I moved to Carlisle and worked in the library there. After the war, he completed his medical training and came back to join what had been his father's practice in Maryport. He moved into his parents' house when they died and Elspeth was installed as the doctor's wife. And they had a family. And I met no-one else. "

"Hard on you."

She shrugged. "Doctors and their wives are important people in any community. Most Cumbrians are simply not comfortable with today's changed attitudes. The village would have been very critical if their doctor had not been loyal to his role and to his marriage and family. Goodness knows what they would have thought if they had known he was not."

"He was not?" Polly was indeed taken aback

"Oh goodness, no" said Veronica with a small smile of pleasure. "Not in the least. Are you shocked?"

"But you said….."

"One day he came into the library."

"And?"

"It was instant. Things grew from there. He had a friend with a flat who was often away. And very occasionally I came here when Elspeth was in hospital with depression. Secretly of course. She never liked living here."

"And Alice knew," Polly guessed.

"You have it. Elspeth eventually was in hospital permanently. She used to clean for him and, yes, she suspected I am sure, although she was loyal to Robert."

"Wasn't that very daring of you? And your husband too?"

"We had waited a long time."

"Sad," said Polly.

During a long silence Polly went on painting, Veronica eventually continued.

"When we were our age, we couldn't put things off any longer but I don't expect you to know that."

"I think I can."

Veronica looked at her closely for a moment.

"You can have no idea," she said, "of the feelings of an older woman when she is really in love."

Polly stopped painting and held her brush in the air. "Yes I do," she said quietly.

"My dear," said Veronica, "I didn't mean that as a question. How thoughtless of me." After more silence, she said "I did wonder, my dear, if you were running away or otherwise you perhaps would have gone back by now. Am I right?"

"Oh yes, you are," said Polly with a sigh.

"Shall I guess or do we leave it there?" said Veronica.

"I would be glad to tell you. In fact I think I need to tell someone. Shall we have a drink first?"

Polly got out two glasses, tumbled ice in from the freezer

and poured them both a whisky. She had been drinking rather more of it recently. With the sun glinting on their glasses in the sunset, she at last began to tell her own story, thinking she would pace it as Veronica had done, but instead it fell from her like a waterfall.

"I did fall in love. I did have a secret affair. And then he was killed in a car crash last November."

"You poor woman!" She paused. "And you came here to grieve."

Polly nodded.

"And you have a family?"

"A husband and two grown up children – well nearly grown up."

"And do they know?"

Polly shook her head.

"Does your husband know?" Polly shook her head.

"And you had been keeping this love affair totally secret?" Polly nodded.

"For how long?"

"For over a year and then since his death three months ago."

"You poor woman," Veronica said again. She moved across to Polly to comfort her and the two of them moved to the sofa. That she might receive, let alone deserve, any sympathy released Polly's tears. But she knew that unlike her new friend, she was not able to feel good about having had an affair, although she might once have felt and behaved as if she deserved the freedom to do so. Until Tom died. And now she had no idea how she ought to feel.

Gradually her tears subsided and she murmured the half-remembered words of a hymn she had sung at school…..

"…..the clouds you so much dread…."

Veronica completed the verse,

"are big with mercy…..and shall break in blessings on your head. William Cowper! 'God moves in a mysterious way.'

"No blessings though," Polly said sadly.

"Well, there will be one day. You are still young. At some point you will know what to do next?"

Polly nodded and another long silence followed, broken by Veronica.

"I'm glad you wanted to paint me."

"So am I. Thank you." Polly found her handkerchief and went back to her easel.

"Shall we carry on with this portrait another time?" Veronica said, standing up.

Chapter Six

On Monday, 19th March 221 fresh cases were reported in the area, some in West Cumbria.

Monday, March 19th

"Why does it need a bloody professor to convince them!"
Jim's fiercest outburst so far came late on Tuesday evening, when they were watching "Newsnight."   Some professor said that the situation was out of control and some brigadier said that local knowledge was not being sufficiently used. And that did it! Jim was up on his feet banging about the room cursing and swearing at the government, at MAFF, at the ignorance of the Ministry vets who he wouldn't let near his farm if he could help it, at the drivers who went to the wrong farms, at the latest announcement that culling would take place on suspicion alone! Jim bounded from his chair, yelling at the top of his voice.

"What's wrong with vaccination, eh? If they go on like this they'll have to get the army in! It's a f…..ng disaster all right and they're making things f….ng worse! Contradicting themselves all the time so we don't know where we are. Can't trust anyone any more. Bunch of fools and incompetents, the whole f…ng lot of them."

Ethel found his swearing hard at the best of times but it got louder and cruder until Jonty stepped in to steady him down a bit. And then Jim turned on him. No bloody use he was as a son, thinking he could take over with his stupid computer, sitting there all day. Was that was farming was coming to…. and so on and so on. Jonty defended the computer as the modern way and that sent Jim off again.

F….ng computers! F…ng modern farming!"
And then it began to get physical. Jim was lashing out and Jonty was dodging about, ducking blows that were meant for the air or the door or anything in his way until there was a mighty crash and the dresser, full of her willow-patterned plates came crashing down onto the floor.

"Now look what you've done, you old fool," shouted Jonty and Jim just let rip and punched him hard on the chin, drawing blood, and then banged out of the room and the house, slamming the door behind him so that the whole house shook. Ethel could hear him shouting in the yard. The dogs woke up and joined in and she wondered who might be passing down the road to hear. Ethel and Jonty stood there looking at each other until she got a cloth from the kitchen and made him sit down in the mess while she mopped up the blood from his face.

"He always had a good left hook," said Jonty ruefully.

"When is it all going to end?" said Ethel near to tears. " and don't you make it worse by spending so much time on that computer or nosing around Mrs Creed or your Dad'll kill you"

"You worry too much about me, Mum. Always have."

Ethel nodded her head. "I just hope you don't give me cause."
She bent down and began to pick up her broken plates from the floor, examining how much repairing there was to do, and then together they heaved the dresser up back into place and rescued all the things that it had swept off the table.

"Let's leave sorting the rest out until the morning, shall us?" he said, putting his arm round her.

"We'll have a cup of tea and go up to bed," said Ethel, tidying a few plates on the dresser.

"Right" said Jonty, " but quick about it. He'll be back and won't want to see me again tonight, that's for sure."

*　　　　　　　*　　　　　　　*

On Tuesday morning, Brian woke up early, recalling with a sinking heart that it was the day to meet again with Ron McNally. How much real power had he been given? The talk of "partnership with schools" was more theoretical than real in his opinion. Schools were far too busy to be equal partners in the education of student teachers. They were dropping out wherever they could. "Not enough time to do the job properly," they were always saying to him. He had to shore things up himself if the students were not simply left to fail. He hated the concept of performance targets - the Department's targets for student numbers, for entry grades, for multi-ethnic entry, for degree results and for continual student evaluations of the teaching staff. Underneath all this free-floating anger he knew he was worrying abnormally about his own performance. What did "performance indicators" really mean? Was his dissatisfaction with his job, with himself, with Polly's terrifying distancing from him, showing through? He was a senior member of staff, had been there almost the longest, sat on all the major committees but yet he was being made to feel a 'failing' member of staff. Max's chat in the bar and his own resulting depression made him fear that he was indeed fast becoming 'a failure'. And it was public. Everyone knew that McNally had been given the prestigious reviewing job and that Brian was his first target.

The corridor on which Brian's department was situated was institutionally long and cream with a drab vinyl floor. It hadn't been decorated for over five years and the floor was scuffed and stained. There was no common room so that staff relationships were conducted either in the general office over the heads of the one or two administrative staff still left sitting at their computers, or in the doorways of each other's offices or up and down the stair-well. Apart from Max's office, all were alike, small and featureless, with one window at the far end through which Brian watched the wagtails strutting on the flat concrete roof outside. His bookshelves were overflowing and papers were piled on the chairs awaiting marking or filing. It was a long time since he could ask any of the diminishing number of young women to file for him.

"Don't worry," Alex, one of his colleagues, called to him, guessing why Brian was early at his desk when he passed his door. "I'd give that young pretender a dose of quiet derision, if I were you."

Brian snorted.

" My turn next remember. Bollocks to it all, Brian. Cheer

up. After all, he is outnumbered."

"You're right," Brian felt a little cheered, "stupid of me to get so rattled."

"We all do, old chap, in these days of bloody outputs and outcomes. It'll all pass. Fashions always do. But why should I care? I've only two years to go before I take early retirement! Roll on the Costa del Sol."

Before he had left the house, Brian had gone upstairs to look at himself in the mirror. He had put on his old green cords, an open-necked woollen check shirt and his dark green pullover with the leather elbow patches that he had stitched on a couple of weeks ago, having tracked down these rare items in the haberdashery department of John Lewis. He had not got round to having his hair cut since Christmas and it was untidy and definitely greying rapidly, though not yet thinning, thank God. However he was noticeably thickening around the waist. He thought of McNally in his tight jeans, regulation polo-necked sweater and trademark black leather jacket. He apparently changed out of his motor-bike leathers into his jeans every morning and came in whistling along the corridors, twirling his helmet as if he were the winner of the Isle of Man TT races. Everyone always knew he had arrived and students, male and female, invariably turned to hail him. What particularly annoyed Brian was McNally's attitude to the sharing out of the hated departmental chores - sorting out timetables, room bookings and being in charge of UCAS applications. The annoying man would constantly refer to his 'childcare' duties as an excuse for not taking on these jobs as if he were the only man around who had ever had a hand in his children's upbringing. He was trying far too hard all the time to epitomise 'the new man' and to respond over-sympathetically, even passionately, to his students' usually exaggerated grievances. He had spearheaded a purge on all the course syllabuses to ensure that anti-this and anti-that and anti-the other got prominence, to the exclusion, so it seemed to Brian, of fundamental educational knowledge and skills. But Max took his cues from the man because he thought he alone had the ear of the students and so Brian had to subject himself to this review. In this defiant mood, he had not changed his clothes but rejoiced to be looking as solid and unexciting as he could. But when he got into his office all such bravado vanished.

He heard McNally whistling before coming to a halt outside his door with an exaggerated slide on the Tuesday morning polished vinyl. He entered cheerily and sat down, moving books and papers from the nearest chair as he did so. Brian faced him, arching his hands to make a stylised triangle with his fingers and thumbs as did Max nowadays.

"For starters, I have made a spreadsheet for us all to fill in," said the younger man enthusiastically, drawing his chair up close to Brian, "and I wonder if, as we agreed, you would look at it before I email it to all." He handed over a paper copy. It was printed in different colours and the font was rather fancy.

"Is that Trebuchet?" said Brian, focussing on the font.

McNally was impressed. "It is actually. My favourite at the moment."

"Is it now? How interesting. Now let me see….."

Through this chink, Brian was able to slip as easily as an otter into water into the role of teacher and guide. He had caught sight of McNally's anxiety about his own performance below his brash exterior. And he, Brian, was always the teacher. Whether it was his son, his daughter, his colleagues or his students, once he had sensed a block or a defence or a tremor, in this case, an attachment to an unimportant detail, the way opened before him - not to dispatch a threat, because the threat was no longer there; nor to win the argument with Max that lay behind the review which was to do with Max losing touch with education. No. The review was the opportunity Brian needed! Through it he might emerge from what younger colleagues -and Polly - saw as his stolid resistance to change. Instead he would re-define for them and himself all that he had ever learnt about how children learn. No new structure or theory or catchword could do its job without connecting to this. He had relied upon it for so long that he had failed to connect it sufficiently to the organisational changes shrouding it from view.

He looked kindly at McNally.

"Ron" he said. "You have something here that is going to be really useful. You have a good basic tool to help us all become clearer about what we are trying to do. While we have to cope with all the political buzz-words in education at the moment, we must see if we can ground them and test them against our own experience in this College. Shall I take it and try to use it myself to see how its format might work in my own area? The phrase 'Partnership with Schools' is the concept meant to be driving what I do, so I will look at this spreadsheet and see how to connect that word with our everyday syllabuses and assessments. Would this be helpful to you, do you think?"

Ron McNally looked startled and then relieved. "That would be very helpful, Brian," he said gravely. "I will leave it with you, shall I, to make any changes you think would improve it?"

"Fine, Ron, give me a week. Is that too long?"

McNally left even more chirpily but with a softer expression on his face. Brian was pleased and looked forward to the opportunity he had created for himself. Then he remembered that his next task was to visit Mrs Marjorie Frost. It was disconcerting to be trusted by the VC for a delicate task at the same time as being put under scrutiny by a chap years his junior.

$$*\qquad\qquad*\qquad\qquad*$$

Polly was restless. Though the loneliness of her grief had been relieved by telling Veronica of it, the ache of loss and the uncertainty about her future were ever-present and adding to despondency about her painting. She wanted to recover her vision of Mellbreak but she could only look at it through her window or from the road and it was mostly hidden in cloud. She listened as usual to the morning news. At least five times a day on Radio Cumbria there was news about the outbreak and it changed a bit every time. Now there were 221 fresh cases and some in West Cumbria. She began to envisage an eventual unfulfilled journey back to London.

The telephone rang and it was Ethel with a shopping list. She told Polly that she was feeling low because there was a row last night. She confessed that she was phoning from the living room having walked through a mess in the kitchen left by a fight between Jim and Jonty which tipped over the dresser. A broken willow plate had just rolled in through the door, she said, after Jim had kicked it there at breakfast. She had been awake most of the night worrying, she said. Getting business-like she dictated the list to Polly and then sighed.

Polly took the cue and said it must be tough. Ethel told her wearily that it was now very likely that the disease would reach them. Wigton had it and the children there were crying over lost animals and sick of the smell of the burning pyres.

"Everyone is trying to keep them away from the worst sights, Mrs Creed, and then it is shown all over the TV."
She loved to hear them shouting in the playground over the fence but she didn't like to think of them watching it all now on TV.

"Even though our school's still open, children from outside the village have stopped coming. Can you still hear them at playtime from where you are?"

"Yes, but not so much as when I was first here," Polly said.

"In case you get to hear them, the men get to shouting now too! Like last night. I was so ashamed! But Jim says we're in a pocket between the outbreak areas, you see. It'll be a miracle if we miss it as it's all down to molecules in the air, Mrs Creed. That's what the farmers are saying. Molecules in the air! No amount of bio-security will stop it -though we must apparently still go on using it."

"I am so sorry. Do you still think it is all right for me to stay?"

"Oh yes," Ethel replied. "Folk are still going into the towns and I am very grateful to you for these bits of shopping. No, it's us on the farms as has got to be careful with the bio-security and that - much use as that might be. And there's me been worrying myself silly about the ducks treading it about when they say it's in the air. But you can't keep every living creature shut up, Mrs Creed. Cows is bad enough any winter, having to change their straw all the time and now they're calving, I can't imagine when the poor things'll get out."

"Any more news from Jim's brother?"

"Mrs Creed. I have never known a man like him cry before. He is sobbing over the phone about what he's lost and what he has had to do and what he has seen. Grown men sobbing, Mrs Creed. You'd never have thought it. Annie, that's his wife, says that one of the disposers – that's them as has to get rid of them – spent three days just chopping cows in half with a bucket swinging from the end of the crane on the front of his tractor, getting them ready for the pyre or burial. Just like some sort of monster, she said. And they all in their bio-security suits like men on the moon. All those years of looking after them silly cows, day and night and it comes to that. Even Jonty's heartbroke and he never wanted to farm in the first place."

*   *   *

When she put the phone down, Polly deemed her own concerns trivial. The roads were scattered with precautionary signs and it seemed obscene for her to drive along them just to look at the countryside. Yesterday she had walked gingerly around the edge of the field beside the barn, just for some fresh air, and on the way back had crossed the lane the children use to get to their playing field. She stood aside while they dashed across, jumping over tree roots, dodging mud and puddles. Some said "Hello missus." You would scarcely guess they were under strain. She especially noticed their shoes – trainers, lace-ups, wellington boots - and had thought how easily contamination could spread. She had made quick drawings of the children running and jumping. Now that she had learnt that it spread in the air, however, it seemed like a medieval plague breathing over the fields and fells.

That she, Polly, was able to offer Ethel support seemed

extraordinary. Her own situation, entirely of her own making, seemed indulgent. The relief of weeping in response to Veronica's kindness could never dispel the lassitude she was slipping back into that was deadening her work. She must stop herself from getting more and more depressed. She must get out. She could drive around at the very least on the main roads. She might even look for a few more sweaters. Retail therapy! The few sweaters she had brought with her were too thin and impossible to get dry.

"Everyone's looking for the same," said the woman in the sheepskin shop. Try Marks and Spencers."

Shopping was so easy in South London. 'I'll just pop to Marks and Spencer's,' she would say. But she took up the suggestion and drove towards one of the coastal towns. She'd seen the sea the first evening she arrived and never since. The roads became wider and she overtook several lorries. She followed the signs into the town and found a parking place. She got out of the car, pulling her anorak around her, and stepped straight into a large puddle. She swore and looked uneasily around her realizing that this was an industrial town.

"My God," she muttered, "this place needs an uplift too." The houses and shops were similar to those she now knew well in the cosy streets of the inland town, but here they were squashed beside the concrete monstrosities of developers. It was like the worst of South East London. She walked through grey streets until she found a small Marks and Spencer's. She bought a couple of acceptable woollen sweaters and sped back to the car. There must be plenty of poor people around here too, she thought. Not just pretty places. The only brightness came from the wet road before her as she drove off. She recalled that Veronica's father knew well the difference between coastal towns and the inland villages. She passed a forbiddingly black church and longed to get back to the barn and to her easel.

There were intervals in the day now when she did not think of Tom until a sudden flashback stopped her in her tracks. For a moment now, she thought she saw him driving past her in a car the same colour as his, the one he crashed. Once, across the street, she had seen someone with hair styled the same and had wanted to reach out and touch it. She was not safe yet to go home, safe that is, not to give Brian, Jessica and her colleagues reason to wonder what was the matter with her. She had scarcely laughed since Tom's death. By the time she came away, all lively exchanges with her students had ceased. When she tried to make contact to discuss their work, she would become aware of her hollow words. They would move away from her and any buzz present in the studio would either be suppressed or would exclude her. She found making decisions about ordering paint, canvasses and other materials, exhausting and had ended up ordering what she had ordered the last time and then only after spending an unnecessary amount of time trying to find the right order forms.

She was thinking thus when she began to be uneasy about her whereabouts. She did not recognise what she was passing nor any of the names on the signposts. She stopped to look for the map but of course she had forgotten to put it back after last night's conversation with Ethel when she had fetched it to look up the location of Wigton. She saw a sign to Maryport and half remembered that she was too far north. She passed a row of terraced houses facing the road, backing on to a stony beach and a grey sea. 'If I wanted to paint depression,' she thought, "this would do." She would have to turn right somewhere or turn back. She drove past a sign for 'The Miners' Welfare,' and saw another to 'The Moor'. She thought of Veronica. Signalling to the lorry behind her she turned off in that direction glimpsing the driver shout abuse at her. She shrugged. She would just have to keep on going and going, away from the coast. At the next cross-roads, after passing a patch of woodland, she kept straight on. The land was rising gradually and was getting moor-like and very bleak. 'Must be somewhere near Veronica,' she thought and was briefly encouraged that she could be on the right track. However, she was soon experiencing a growing level of panic. Then round a corner, she saw a big notice. A large red triangle with an exclamation mark in the middle of it and in large letters.

DISEASE PRECAUTIONS

And below it in white letters on a red square

Strictly
NO ENTRY

She stopped, her brakes screeching, and wound down the window. Then she smelt it. And heard it. Over the hedge on her right in the distance in the middle of a large field was the orange-red brilliance and roaring noise of a huge fire. She had stumbled upon the one thing she should not have encountered. She sat in the car in shock. recalling what Ethel had told her about the pyres and the school children in Wigton. By mistake, she had found one. She was ashamed of herself for her carelessness and absent-mindedness. Then her shame changed to appalled fascination at what she could see and smell and hear. She sat riveted to the spot, peering from the open car-window through the gateway into the field. After a quarter of an hour of silent watching, she reached into the dashboard compartment and fetched out her sketchpad. She was struck by the bizarre shapes of animal legs sticking out of the pyre at crazy angles and the huge movements of the men with pitchforks stoking the blaze. She drew quickly and then roughly crayoned colours on top of her pencil lines to suggest the raw brilliance.

After sketching the fells in the background and the men in the foreground and the fire from different angles, she put away her pad and started the engine, turned the car round and drove slowly back. Visual excitement was tempered by a sense of horror at the enormity of what she had witnessed. She was in a desperate state to get back to the barn lest her mind's eye lose the essence of what she had seen. She could almost see it on the canvas already. Instead, she had to force herself to concentrate on finding her way back to the privacy of the barn.

* * *

Brian drove into the Frosts' driveway in the early afternoon, even more apprehensive than on his first visit. He noted again the affluent style of the house and garden and this time, recalled that there was also a flat in London. Marjorie had obviously been waiting for him and they settled down as before in the living room, he in the same chair. She served him tea as before.

"Mrs Frost," he began.

"Marjorie please and it is Brian isn't it?"

Brian nodded and began again. "Marjorie, the Vice-Chancellor has asked me to explore a little with you some of Tom's contacts outside the College."

He dreaded her asking him why the Vice Chancellor wanted to know such things to which he had rehearsed a very vague answer. Instead she asked the simple question.

"What do you want to know?"

He felt rude and abrupt as he cut straight to the nub of the Vice-Chancellor's enquiry.

"Well, for example, could we have the name of his solicitor do you think?"

Again she did not ask why but rose and went to a small bureau and picked up the address she had already written out. She handed it to him.

"I hope you do not mind my asking for it," he said.

"On the contrary," she replied, "Tom's affairs have turned out to be so complicated that I am quite unable to discuss them myself. His solicitor knows far more about what Brian was involved in than I ever did."

Brian felt uncomfortable. " I see," he murmured.

"I must confess I am not surprised but I do wonder why the College wants to know about his other life. Do you have any idea?" she asked.

"I'm afraid I don't," Brian replied, glimpsing an opportunity to escape without revealing the suspicions about Tom's financial probity.

"Well," she added, "Tom's investments were scattered rather far and wide. I had no idea of the extent and I gather that he moved his money around somewhat too."

"I see,' Brian murmured once more, anxious not to encourage any confessions.

"I might as well tell you," she continued, "though this will not interest the Vice-Chancellor I don't suppose for one minute, that Tom and I led rather separate lives."

"Mrs Frost, Marjorie," he corrected himself. "I do not mean to enquire…."

"Of course you don't, but I am telling you that I now realise that I knew hardly anything of Tom's life, not his College life, his business life, his media life nor his private life although I knew for years that he was having affairs with other women."

Brian was getting more and more embarrassed.

"For example, he never bought paintings for this house and then, strange wasn't it, to find your wife's painting in his flat when I didn't even know he had a flat until I was told and went to collect his clothes."

"I am sorry," Brian mumbled, unsure what he was sorry for – for Polly's painting or Tom's unknown flat or for simply being there as an unhappy reminder.

He stood up. "I had better go."

Marjorie also stood. "There, I have embarrassed you," she said. "You didn't expect to find me telling you things that you don't need or want to hear."

Brian shrugged with his hands and said weakly, "Don't worry about it."

"It is very strange learning more about your spouse at his death than you knew when he was alive," she explained.

"It must be."

"And I can no longer ask him."

"That must make it very difficult for you."

"It does, it does, and I don't want the girls to know that there are things about their father that I can't tell them."

"It must leave you in a very strange position" ventured

Brian.

"Well, at present, for example," she replied, her voice rising as she spoke, "I don't know how much money he had, what his financial commitments were on the flat in London or, so his solicitor tells me, on an apartment he seems to have owned or rented in New York where he did a lot of business, which he seems to have bequeathed to a woman about whom I also knew nothing about nor whether he had committed himself to any further bases in Europe that I suspect he used but have yet to learn about! How do you think that makes me feel, Mr Creed, Brian, I mean?"

Brian was struck dumb. He had no idea how anyone could have lived like this let alone how she might be feeling.

"I'm afraid," she said slowly and emphatically, "Tom was a dealer and a fixer and, maybe since the bubble burst, it is all coming undone, don't you think?" Brian could neither think nor say anything remotely useful.

She concluded her outburst by thanking him for "being understanding" and for taking up his time. She became the calm and sensible widow once more, showing him to the door and saying she hoped that she had been helpful to him and to the Vice-Chancellor. Brian left in a state of shock. He had the information he came for and far more than he wanted to hear. What of all this should he reveal to the Vice Chancellor? He still felt a certain, but diminishing, loyalty to Tom about whom his curiosity was growing apace. He could hardly wait to tell Polly. However he'd better wait until Sunday night or she would accuse him of enjoying scandal-mongering at Tom's expense.

*   *   *

Alice was doing her afternoon walk with the dog just as Polly drove towards the barn.

"She's in a mighty hurry and no getting away from it," she muttered to herself. She saw her skid into the barn entrance and, shortly after, she watched Jonty saunter casually in after her.

"Well, there's a thing," she said.

As she walked on towards the farm, Ethel ran down to the gate to collect the box of shopping.

"Did you see that Ethel?"

"Good Morning Alice," Ethel said, in a hurry to get back to the house.

"Do you want a hand with that box?"

"No thanks Alice." Ethel turned away.

"Did you see what I saw?' said Alice. "That Mrs Creed, you know, your painter lady, skidding away from your gate into her yard and nearly knocking me over and being followed by your Jonty, if I'm not mistaken."

"She's been doing my bit of shopping, Alice." Ethel made light of the information, despite linking it to the fact that Jonty hadn't been in for his dinner.

"Has she then?" said Alice gnomically as usual. "And Jonty gone to thank her for it I expect."

"Happen he has," said Ethel, lifting up the box and walking as briskly as she could up the path. "You get along Alice and mind you keep that dog away from those sacks of disinfectant or Jim'll be after you."

So Alice had seen Jonty after Mrs Creed again! He's a young fool, she thought.

*　　　　　　　*　　　　　　　*

Jonty had woken depressed. He went to the computer as usual and all the information told him the virus was on its way. After the row the previous night, they were in no state to combat a disaster. Jonty was still furious with his father for picking a fight and incensed by his behaviour towards his mother at breakfast this morning. He was fed up with never being able to get away from him, hearing him curse and grumble all day long. He no longer had the freedom to walk across the fields. His father was everywhere – in the sheds, in the barns, changing the straw, cleaning things and then cleaning them again and again. Jonty even thought he was getting like his father, muttering angrily to himself as he went about his jobs, cursing the older man for not letting go his grip on the place and showing no intention of letting him take charge of any part of it, let alone all of it. His father would never retire. He'd die first.

"Does he think I'm not capable of taking over?" And later, "Serve him right if we get the disease here. Serve him bloody right. What do I care!"

Life had got worse from the time that he and his dad had gone to a big farmers' meeting, where his dad had got worked up, making a fool of himself in public, convinced that the government had set things up for an epidemic by storing railway sleepers in readiness for burning sick animals, sacking most of the vets on purpose to destroy the dairy farmers, going on and on about a plot to turn the place into a holiday camp. He thought that was a load of rubbish and had told his dad.

"What d'you want to believe those stories for, you old fool?" he'd said as they were driving home. At least his dad was letting him drive.

"Who're you calling an old fool?" his father had said. "If you think I'm an old fool, get out of the car and I'll drive myself. You don't want to be seen with an old fool!"

He had carried on driving while his father got even more worked up about the government and the minister and the NFU until Jonty put his feet suddenly on the brake and stopped the car with a jerk throwing his dad forward onto the dash board.

"You drive yourself, " he'd shouted at him. "I'll not listen to any more of this."

He had got out, slammed the car door and walked the three miles back home in the dark. Since then they'd not gone anywhere together. The auctions had stopped. No-one dropped into the pub for a crack any more. He was reduced to the computer and telephone calls from his uncle and aunt. He and his Dad knocked about in the farm seeing to the imprisoned animals, having to clean them out, dreading the visits from the vets who came to test them, never knowing when they might have to be taken off and slaughtered. Life had turned into drudgery and ended up with a f….g fight!

He went back into the house once during the morning, not wanting, in his current black mood, to meet either of his parents. On impulse, he took a bottle of whisky from the cabinet. By the end of the morning, still seething with anger, he had taken more than a few swigs until he knew he'd better not go home for his dinner. Then, opportunely, he thought, just as he rounded the corner of the loning, he saw Polly drive into her entrance and decided to follow her – to get a cup of coffee and a biscuit at least.

*   *   *

Polly had dropped off Ethel's shopping at the gate, narrowly avoiding Alice and her dog and scraping the car wing just missing the stone wall. She hurried into the barn. She was still in the grip of the burning pyre, anxious to begin to prepare a canvas big enough and get colours and shapes quickly down on paper first. She threw the plastic bag of jumpers and her drawing pad hastily on the kitchen table along with her car keys and rang at once to tell Ethel to look out for the shopping in the usual place. As she put the phone down there was a knock at the door. To her dismay and frustration, there stood Jonty. Now was not the time to talk about his painting! He asked to come in and then, to her surprise, pushed to come in. He smelt of drink. Reluctantly she stepped aside to let him pass. She recalled Ethel's account of the fight between Jim and Jonty.

"Aren't you going to offer me some of that coffee?" he asked, leaning against the kitchen counter. This was a different Jonty. She was immediately on her guard. Without replying, she moved to switch on the kettle, making sure she did not brush against him as she squeezed her way to the sink. But at that moment he caught sight of the sketch-pad open on the table at a sketch of the pyre. He picked it up and waved it in the air.

"Well! Look at this then!" he said, "Fancy you going out

of your way to look at a pyre of dead animals. Going to paint it now, I suppose, disgraceful though it is to some of us. It's not f…..g scenery to paint!"

She began to explain. "You have me wrong…." but knew at once that he wouldn't listen to any explanation in his present state. Instead she held out her hand for the pad.

Tipsy and emboldened, he saw his advantage and held the pad high above his head like a child snatching a toy in the playground.

"I think you had better give me that, " she said.
Still holding the pad aloft with one arm, he got his other arm roughly round her waist. His tone softened as he pulled her close to him.

"I thought we were friends."
Pressed to his chest, she could smell the whisky. When she tried to push him away, he held her more tightly. He was vastly stronger than she was and bent close to her in an attempt to kiss her. She turned her face away.

"Jonty," she said in an urgent whisper. "Jonty, please let me go!"

He flipped the pad sideways onto the table and, still holding her close, stroked her hair with his free hand.

"I'll not hurt thee. You've lovely hair. I've wanted to touch it for a long time. Did you know that?"

She stayed very still, her eyes averted, trying not to provoke him, thinking only of how to escape. But his hand moved from her hair to take hold of her chin so that he was able to turn her face towards him and hold it close.

"I expect you knew I had my eyes on you," he murmured. "They say a woman always knows when a man fancies her, and with you being here on your own, no husband, or none around, and you a modern woman, why not let me give you a kiss?"

"Jonty," she said again, "please let me go."

"I'll be gentle with you," he coaxed, "I may be a farmer but I can be very soft."

As he put out his lips to touch hers, she moved her face

quickly to one side with the effect that, being unsteady, he overbalanced and failed to make contact, though he still held her fast to his chest.

Then the sudden sound of a dog barking outside on the road broke the tension. He loosened his hold and lurched away from her. Polly reached for the edge of the table to steady herself and put her hand on the drawing pad. When she realised where her hand was, she feared that this would arouse him again but he kept his distance, looking at the pad and then at her, with hurt in his eyes. He began shaking his head as if to wipe out what had occurred.

"That'll make a fine painting," he said quietly. "It is after all what everything is about - loss and waste and bloody mistakes!"

He lurched towards the door and grabbed and yanked at it making it shudder open across the flagstones. He went out leaving the door to bang shut behind him. Polly hauled herself up on the kitchen stool her eyes fixed on the door.

*   *   *

On the drive over for her afternoon sitting, Veronica was thinking about the turn in the friendship with this younger woman, savouring the relationship of sitter and painter. People of her age were renowned for telling strangers their life stories but she hadn't expected that Polly would confide hers in return. She had been very moved, remembering words from a Bob Dylan song from the 1960s – 'She walks just like a woman, but she breaks just like a girl'. Polly was a beautiful woman. She could understand men wanting her. She wondered about the circumstances leading her to embark on an affair. While Polly studied her closely, so had she been observing Polly. She betrayed an unexpected shyness at times which made Veronica realise that she was not as confident as she first thought. Sometimes beautiful women develop a protective covering to guard against too much intimacy. Yet when she swung her long hair away from her eyes, it was not difficult to imagine this attracting any man. She might be unaware of her power to attract. In a community like Milnethwaite, it was still the custom for women of her age to be settling into middle age whereas Polly still dressed youthfully. That was why she had warned her to be careful of Jonty.

Veronica drove into the barnyard. She got out and knocked at the door. Receiving no answer, she peered through the window. Though the room was illuminated with a slanting ray of sunshine, she could see no sign of Polly. She walked out onto the road and looked up and down to see if she had just walked out in the afternoon sunshine. Then she saw Alice with her dog.

"Nice afternoon now it's come out," Alice called.

"Good afternoon, Alice," Veronica replied, "We could do with a bit of sunshine."

"We could that." Alice joined her at the entrance to the barn. "Looking for the painter lady are you?"

"She'll be somewhere here about," Veronica said. "Her car's here."

"I reckon she's there all right," said Alice. "In a hurry too, judging by the car. She's had that Jonty around again and all. Leastways I saw him leave in a hurry too. I guess he wouldn't want Jim to know as he pops in there from time to time."

"I'll knock again." Veronica was not going to encourage Alice to say more.

"Don't you worry," said Alice reading her thoughts, "I shan't be telling anyone he's been," and walked off through the churchyard full of her own counsel.

Veronica went back into the yard and looked again through the window and now saw Polly perched awkwardly on the kitchen stool, her shoulders hunched and her hands held tightly together between her knees. She quietly pushed the door open and went in. Polly looked up, then jumped up and fell upon her shoulders.

"Thank God it's you!"

"My dear, who did you think it might be?"

"Jonty."

"What on earth has happened? What has he done?"

"Only made a pass at me."

'Oh no. I feared as much? Did he....?"

"No, no. Nothing came of it …..but, I began to think was going to."

Veronica guided Polly to the sofa and sat down beside her, holding both her hands in hers to absorb some of her evident distress. Polly described briefly what had happened.

"I don't know what to say," said Veronica at the end. " I was afraid he might get the wrong idea but I did not for one moment imagine he would try anything on."

"It must be me. I must have given him the wrong idea."

Veronica sighed. "No, no, I'm sure not. But I know him a little and hear about him from others. He has had one or two unhappy relationships and has been without a girl for a very long time. He is a normal man after all - not that behaving as he has is normal of course."

Polly said she had been trying to work out how it had happened. He had been persistent in trying to see her before, yes, but never pushy. She had thought of him as diffident and shy. With students she was used to keeping relationships friendly but professional. Some did get crushes on her, but she had never been caught out as today.

"He seemed to think I was available because I am a 'modern' woman with no husband around, as if that made me fair game."

Veronica commented, "Many men in these parts probably share that view."

"And the strange thing is" Polly added, "that he didn't know the truth – that I had once made myself available."

"No," Veronica said firmly. "No. You must not blame yourself. It sounds to me as if you did very well to calm him down and you must simply not make those connections. Your relationship with the man you told me you had loved has nothing whatever to do with Jonty wanting to kiss you. You can't help being beautiful. Jonty would be bound to find you so too, poor man."

"And he was drunk."

"Ah. I see."

In a few moments, she added, "Now what are we going to do about it?"

"What can I do? Keep the door locked? I am a grown woman, I should be able to deal with such things."

"You are sounding hard on yourself again! Now stop it!" said Veronica and rose to find the whisky. This time it was she who poured Polly a drink.

Polly slowly repeated the last words Jonty had said as he left the barn. 'Loss, waste and mistakes. That is what he said everything is about."

"Well, mistake certainly!" Veronica said. "I grant you he may be having a hard time of it. All the farmers are, but that is no excuse for trying to force himself on you."

She sat down and clapped her hands indicating decision time. "What about coming back with me for the night?"

"No, no. I'm sure he won't come back."

"I should think he is by now very ashamed of himself," said Veronica. "He should be. But I expect you will feel shaky for a bit."

"Thanks for the offer," said Polly, in the doorway, "but I'll be fine."

*   *   *

Once alone, Polly put on the lights and drew the curtains and sank back again onto the sofa. She was exhausted. She had been jolted out of depression into a blaze of horror on the moor and then confronted by Jonty's clumsy attempt to kiss her. It was almost laughable. She'd been so wrapped up in her own concerns that, though wary of him, she had never thought for a moment that he might be having fantasies about her or that he would try to act on them. Yet she became aware of a strong physical reaction to being held so tightly by him. Veronica had roundly repudiated the idea that she could have encouraged him but she could not rid herself of the sensation of his body and the thought that that she had attracted him. She felt cheapened by it, feeling a level of disgust not with him but with herself.

In an effort to dispel it, she switched on the television news. The lead story was that, by mistake, a herd of cows had been culled on a farm nearby. They'd got the map reference wrong, had turned up, culled them and found out their mistake later. Perhaps Jonty had seen that on the news before calling on her and that had contributed to his railing against 'loss, waste and bloody mistakes.'

She had a shower and went early to bed but knew as soon as she lay between the sheets, that she wouldn't sleep. The event had served to re-connect her unwillingly to her sexuality. While Tom was alive, it had been hard going home to sleep beside Brian, but to sleep beside him after Tom's death had been unendurable. A few times they made love and she had then lain awake in a state of utter bleakness. She knew she had to get away. Now, Jonty's advances had forced her to feel a woman again. She lay sobbing and repeating Tom's name. He had been courteous, gentle and fun and never in doubt that she would yield. And this set off a new train of thought.

How had she been so easily seduced by such a sexually confident man?

Chapter Seven

On 22nd March the Government's Chief Scientific Adviser proposed the contiguous cull policy in the Cabinet Office Briefing Room at its first meeting chaired by the Prime Minister. Sheep within 3km of infected premises in the Carlisle/Solway area were to be slaughtered within 48 hours.

Tuesday, March 20th

Jonty left the barn in a highly agitated state. He blundered into the farmyard with tears in his eyes. It was three o'clock in the afternoon and they began milking at four o'clock. He and his Dad always did this together these days to keep a check on the cows. So, they'd have to meet. He must find something to do to keep out of his sight until he had pulled himself together and sobered up. Not that he was drunk any more. More upset than anything, more cast down, or cast aside more like.

The dogs came up to lick his hand. He'd take them for a run. He whistled to them and led them out along the muddy road into the top field on the outskirts of the village. The wind was strong and he climbed slowly behind the dogs up to the crags at the top of the field where the wind was at its strongest, buffeting him almost off his feet. From there he could see across to the fells. He'd loved this spot as a boy, bringing the dogs up and clambering roughly over the rocks, imagining himself escaping and hiding from an enemy that was chasing him up the hill. He squatted on a boulder, trying to make sense of what had just happened. He thought she liked him. They were getting on well. Anything might have gone on to happen. He'd thought he would show her a few places, like this. He'd help her over the rocks and he'd hold her hand to steady her and…. and then Foot and Mouth had arrived. Every time he had thought about her since, he had recalled her perfume the day she had mended the computer, his hand brushing against her soft wool jumper and her hair, always her hair. He had dared to think that she was lonely and wanted him too. He looked out for her bedroom light at night and in the early mornings clinging to the possibility that she fancied him but that she was being careful, like he was, on account of his mother. Always on the phone, they were, his mother going on and on, the way women do. He brooded over why she was not at home with her husband and daughter. Who else had he to think about nowadays to know that he was alive? A stunning woman appearing like that into his life. All he did was to sip a drop of whisky to give himself some hope. Now he knew she had been humouring him all along.

He stood on top of the bare crags, the wind tugging and beating the his old coat around his legs, and felt a rush of shame at what he had done. From wanting a bit of notice from her, he'd gone mad for her. When he'd seen that she had drawn one of the pyres, as if she were there to make money out of them like outsiders always did, he'd grabbed the drawing pad and then….the memory flooded over him; the woman he'd looked at, marvelled at and thought about night and day for months. If it weren't for Alice's bloody dog barking, he might have tried to go further and, now he thought with shame, he would have made even more of a fool of himself. As if there were a knife twisting inside him, he was in an agony of remembering. He cried out into the wind.

"You f…..ng idiot," he shouted. "You've done it now!"
Eventually he wrapped his coat around him, called out to the dogs and set off down the hill through the field to the cowsheds. There was his Dad already started. They said not a word to one another but got on with the task, pushing and patting and shouting at the cows, who bumped and banged about and bellowed like old women as the milking clusters were fitted onto them - the beasts that they'd be bound to lose one day soon.

The following day, remembering that dog bark that Polly hadn't seemed to hear, he couldn't shift the thought that Alice might have seen him at the barn, looked through the window and would tell his mother. So he kept himself out of sight, bent over the computer perusing the farming websites, nervously looking up 'Polly Creed' on Google to find a photograph of her, one or two paintings she had done and a list of all she did. It was amazing. A photograph on the web was all he would ever have of her now.

At the next meal-time, to prove how busy he'd been, he recited to his father all the facts he had learnt that day.

"They're fetching in vets from Ireland."

"That's because they got rid of them on purpose."

"Dad that's rubbish."

"It's part of the government's plan. They can't fool me!"

"They only expected a tenth of the cases. That's why."

"Don't believe it!"

"They are going ahead with contiguous culls." This was Jonty's prize fact, knowing that Jim had been arguing against them. "It says on the website that this had created a climate of confrontation in Cumbria."

"Bloody fools," Jim raged. "that way they reckon they'll get to us after all. That's what they want! Even if we don't get it, they'll have our cows nonetheless because the poor bloke's cows next door get it." He'd then march about the room in anguish. " What's the point of taking care with all this f….ng bio-security! It's in the bloody air, for God's sake. It'll have us one way or another!"

Relations between Jonty and his father were still in a precarious state when a phone-call came that crushed them both and threatened to throw even Ethel off balance. Ethel took the call. She screamed out Eric's name so loudly that Jim and Jonty both came rushing into the living room.

"Eric has taken his own life" she cried and then turned back to Annie on the other end of the line. "Oh No, Oh No! Don't tell me Annie. Not that! Not Eric!" She turned to them again. "It's Eric. He's dead."

Jim seized the telephone and heard Annie try to explan

"He's killed himself, Jim. Your little brother. He's gone! Hadn't slept for a week. He said he'd never get over it and he was right. He hasn't!"

"Annie! Annie!" Jim wailed into the phone.

 "It was seeing all his beloved animals lying about in a rotting pile in the corner of a field after they were shot, stinking, they were, " she continued.

"Annie, Annie," Jim wailed again..

"They were there for days before they took them to be buried."

Jim was white with shock and anguish. Ethel stood close beside him and Jonty sat on the sofa with his head in his hands. Jim held the phone away from his ear and loudly whispered "He's topped himself." Then he staggered as if to fall. Ethel immediately took the phone from him and Jonty caught him and led him to his chair. All his own bitterness was forgotten as shock and grief took hold. Jonty went to the drinks cupboard to pour him a whisky.

"Annie, Annie!" Ethel said and asked how he'd done it.

"Shot himself," Ethel repeated to Jim and Jonty.

"Aye, he would," wailed Jim. "that's how he'd do it all right"

"What can we do?" Ethel asked Annie.

"Nothing anyone can do. The police are coming."

"Are you on your own? Can we drive over?"

"It's dark," said Jonty. "They can't stop us at this time of night."

"I should have hidden the gun," Anne said, " I should have thought!"

"We'll come straight there. Never mind the restrictions," Ethel said " We'll come. This is family."

"I'll drive," said Jonty.

"No you *won't*," growled Jim.

Ethel put her hand over the telephone explaining to Annie that Jim was speaking to her.

"We'll not be going and that's that. We'll take no risks with spreading foot and mouth. Eric wouldn't want that and I won't have it, do you hear? We'll wait until we can give him a proper funeral. Then we'll go. Tell her that Ethel."

"Annie. I'm so sorry. Jim says we can't come on account of the restrictions."

There was more talking until the police arrived and Ethel put the phone down.

She began to think aloud. "Who will look after Annie? What will the police do now? Will there have to be an inquest? Will the funeral be held because of the restrictions? Surely we'll be allowed over for that?"

"Stop wittering woman!" said Jim, taking charge. "Annie's daughter and her kids will go over to be with her."

"If they go, Dad, they'll have to stay on in the house."

"You think I don't know that! It's a bloody war. And my own brother dead along with his beasts."

*   *   *

That night, Ethel sat up in bed waiting for Jim to come up and get in beside her. He was late coming. She was so worried about where he was that she got up to look. When she got downstairs in her dressing gown she found him in the living room in his chair, looking straight ahead of him. He took no notice of her when she joined him.

"Are you coming to bed?"

Ethel put her hand on his arm, half expecting him to push it off. He wasn't one to accept sympathy even from her. This time he didn't seem to notice it.

"I shan't sleep," he said.

"You've got to try."

He sat in profound silence and she sat in her chair the other side of the fireplace, the way they always did last thing before they turned in for bed. Not like tonight, when he hadn't followed her up.

Eventually, without looking up, he said," I wish it were me and not him."

"Aye, I know what you mean."

"He was always my little brother and I always looked out for him."

"I know you did."

"It's all because I'm the older one that I got this farm and he had to move away. And now he's lost everything. It's not right.

It should have been me as went and then I'd have got the trouble. I should have got it not him."

"You can't think that. Think of Jonty."

"Jonty don't want the farm," Jim grunted, "he'd be glad to lose it all."

"That's not fair. He'd not leave you now."

"That's as may be but Eric couldn't cope, you see. He's not as strong as me. Never was."

"You've got a son to carry on. Poor Eric and Annie hadn't no-one but their daughter. That's what we've got to do."

"I'd as soon give it all up the way I am now. Let Jonty get out if that's what he wants."

"You've got to pick up the pieces and carry on. You've got to get through all this and then we'll see."

"I can't do it, Ethel."

"You'll have to let Jonty help you. He's not like you, but he cares. I know that. You know that."

"Do I?"

At that point, Jim heaved himself out of his chair and went upstairs, leaving Ethel to turn off the lights. When she got into the bedroom, he was curled up already with his face turned to the wall. He wasn't going to give way any more to anybody, any night or any day, she thought. He would suffer on his own, in his own way, as he always did, he with his wretched pride. He would be picturing his brother, the only friend of his life, with whom he'd gone through childhood under the task-master that was their father. He was going to miss him for the whole of the rest of his life from now on. They'd kept things going for the sake of the family tradition and now he had to do it alone. He would go on thinking that Jonty wouldn't follow him even though he'd been hard on him just to keep him from going soft. But he'd have to ease up with the lad now, after this. It was Ethel who stayed awake that night listening to Jim eventually snore.

    *   *   *

The following morning, Ethel rang to tell Polly the dreadful news.

"Jim wouldn't go over there yesterday, but I would have gone," said Ethel, "despite everything, I'd have gone, Mrs Creed. Jonty would have driven me, but Jim was adamant. He'd take no risks or his name would be dirt, he said. His own brother, Mrs Creed!"

Ethel talked on, telling Polly more of how they had heard the news, how Jim took it and how he'd nearly collapsed. Then she suddenly stopped because Jim and Jonty had come in for their break.

Polly was moved with pity. After a while, she fetched the largest canvas she had brought with her and laid it on the easel lengthways. She had to paint. She had to do something to express herself. On a large pad, she began to map out the overall scheme for the pyre, drawing swirling, vigorous, broad shapes. By the afternoon she had a draft in place and turned to the canvas, anxious not to lose from her mind's eye, the picture from the day before. With a soft pencil she blocked in the background to the extraordinary surreal vision she had seen. Here was the shape of the moor rising like a great whale in front of the fells. Here was the grey sea and the mean houses built almost onto the beach. She traced out the shape of the fire with legs sticking up at obscene angles out of a fiery furnace tended by dark figures pushing cattle into the flames. It was as vicious as any medieval Doom painting she had ever seen. When dusk fell, it was all roughly blocked in. She stopped and stepped away to look at it. This was a painting she could not, would not rush.

That night she had a horrendous nightmare. Images of burning and dying were swirling around her; live animals on fire; dark men with pitchforks, sometimes figuring Jonty, sometimes his father and sometimes a dead man with a gun in his hand; children were running helter-skelter down fell-sides as if being chased into the fiery pit, and, in the midst of the chaos, was Tom trapped and dying in his car. Since she had listened at the inquest to the account of his death, she had outlawed the details of his broken bones and torn flesh, entangled with metal but now images of his smashed body invaded her half-sleeping, half-waking state, mixed up with images of dead cattle.

The following morning, as soon as it was light enough, she rose from her troubled sleep and went to the canvas. She began slowly building up the painting. She could hear again the gunshot sounds of the fire burning and the men's coarse voices shouting. She could hear the bellowing of the cattle, though in truth they were dead and decaying in great battlefield heaps long before they reached their destruction. And she could smell the stinking, cloying, poisonous odour of the burning contaminated flesh that, it was said, hung about the moorland sites for days and nights making people distraught with despair for miles around.

Over the next few days, blazes of thick, vivid paint would irradiate the piled up black shapes of stiff flesh and cracking bones, lodging and dislodging continually as the burning fire shifted and flared around them. She painted children and women running away from the scourge. And in the midst she painted Tom, looking at her out of the fire.

*   *   *

Jonty had not seen Polly since his disastrous visit to the barn though he still kept an eye on her window night and morning. When his uncle had topped himself, Jonty had watched his father's violent reaction, thinking, as he'd caught him when he fell, that he would die from the shock. Compassion welled up and he thought of his father as he had thought of him when a young boy – he had been a strong man, pig-headed but wise. Though the new-found compassion wavered in the face of his father's stubborn refusal to go to his aunt's side, it turned to respect for his stubborn adherence to his farming priorities and his local reputation. He would not risk his herd or his neighbours' getting the virus. He was a farmer first and last. Jonty began to believe that he stood in a strong succession and ought to feel proud of it. In the days that followed, the regular chores of feeding and milking created a new reverence for life as, father and son, they worked at their trade side by side in silence. The silence was no longer full of resentment but of grief.

Sitting alone one evening after his father and mother had gone to bed, remorse over Polly returned. His parents' sorrow had been prising him away from his own miseries. He knew he had insulted Polly. She had stayed calm all the while he was trying to kiss her. Her dignity left him weak with love of her. Muddled by the whisky, he had even believed she was going to make money out of painting the fire. He recalled her total lack of retaliation. She had relied solely on her quietness to shame him and it had. He would never deserve such a woman.

Eventually he went to the living room, avoiding the computer and going instead to his mother's bureau to find a fountain pen and some writing paper. He was no scholar, so his first attempt at writing a letter looked child-like and naïve. He stuck at the task however and eventually penned a note that was as good as he could manage.

Dear Mrs Creed,

I am very sorry for coming on to you the other day. It was a terrible thing to do and you do not deserve it. I am very ashamed and ask you to forgive me though I know you never could. Drink is no excuse. It made me do what I wanted to do but not in the way I ever wanted to do it. I think you are a wonderful, beautiful person and you should not have some stupid brute like me treating you like I did.

I shall not visit you again or do anything else to bother you. I hope your painting turns out all right. It should be very good.

Yours faithfully,

Jonty Stewart

PS My uncle has committed suicide on account of losing all his animals. These are bad times.

He waited until her light went off and delivered it before going to bed, putting on his wellie boots to avoid making any noise to wake her as he crossed her yard.

*   *   *

Polly found Jonty's note and sat reading it over breakfast. It was from the shy man she had first thought Jonty to be. She pushed her chair back from the table and stretched her legs. She was glad he had written. She had counselled herself not to blame herself and had at times had blamed him, but now she felt sorry for him. He had said he wouldn't trouble her again and she believed him. She would think how best to reply.

*   *   *

Marjorie watched Brian turn out of the drive before going indoors to clear away the tea things. So, there was trouble at the College too. At her request, his solicitor had taken away all the papers from Tom's desk and the computer and filing cabinet. He had subsequently telephoned to warn her that getting probate would take a long time. Tom's properties, the companies on whose boards he sat, his media contracts and own stocks and shares were 'a more varied portfolio than was usual for a university professor,' he had said. He advised her to consult her bank, which should be in a position to help her with 'any transitional difficulties'. The Bank Manager had, to her surprise, offered to come to her house to advise her. His visit, however, had caused her more alarm than comfort. She learnt that Tom had of course many accounts of which she had known nothing.

"One of my staff, a special adviser who handles large

accounts," he said, "has been keeping an eye on his affairs for some time. Did you know this?"

Marjorie shook her head. "I thought that might be the case," he said nodding sagely.

How she disliked men being inscrutable in pretence of being kind. When she asked whether this member of staff was Tom's adviser or was actually investigating him, she was given a non-committal answer about 'certain inconsistencies.' The bank manager then admitted, when she challenged him on the strength of the solicitor's information, that Tom had transferred a flat in New York to a named woman and that the special adviser had indeed also learnt of 'other liaisons with possible financial implications.'

"It must have been a way of securing his investments" he said, " very unusual."

Her abrupt response to this was to ask him and his staff to deal in future with Tom's solicitor over all matters that did not directly concern her.

Overcome with a wish to get away as fast as she could from any more obfuscation, she rose and said firmly that she intended to sell the house quickly and move to York. Instead of rising too, he slowly shook his head and explained, as if to a child, that she could do nothing before probate was granted. So she stood there, humiliated. She was stuck, with no idea of how much money she had at her disposal, paying out unnecessary money for the girls' education and staying on in a house that no longer felt remotely like a home.

In recollecting this ghastly man's visit and realising from Brian that the College was now also involved, anger was an insufficient description of her feelings about Tom. She raged at him for leaving her in a state of ignorance about her financial situation and for placing her at the mercy of 'advisers' who would feather their own nests at her expense; at herself for yielding to his wishes for their daughters' lives; for not divorcing him over the first woman, let alone all the others she had guessed at but known nothing of. With dismay she saw that her bitterness had so alienated her from him over the years that she had in effect allowed, even encouraged, his betrayals.

*   *   *

In the last hours of the working week, Miles had still not heard from Sue though he had left daily messages at her flat and at work. Jess'd come to give him a hard time and Sue had walked in to hear her. He made a final call to Sue at work number and was told she had already set off for Leeds. He was so desperate to see her that he decided to meet her at King's Cross where she went to catch her usual train. Afraid to miss her, he took a taxi realising that he might already be too late. Having promised the taxi driver twice the usual fare if he got him to the five fifty train in time he sat on the edge of his seat in a state of high anxiety, watching the clock and the fare, as the driver took one back street cut-through after another. Then he ran fast into the station hall, dodging the Friday night crowds and banging into commuters as he went. The departure board showed that the train had not yet left the platform. He squeezed past the ticket barrier hastily looking in at the windows as he ran along the train. He reached the last but one carriage, where she usually sat, without seeing her and, breathing heavily, began to make his forlorn way back when he saw her, running along the platform towards him. They practically bumped into each other. Running beside her, he took her bag from her hands and grabbed the last remaining open door so that she could clamber up the step, handing her the bag just as the porter came along to shut the door, his whistle in his mouth and the flag in his hand.

Sue was astonished to see him. "Thanks for the bag," she said as the door shut her off from him. "I'll ring you from my mobile and explain."
The train moved off past him leaving him looking down on the track and he joined the troop of left-over bystanders walking unhurriedly away. He would have a drink at the station bar and then walk home. Holding on to his mobile in his pocket, onto the

hope it represented, he was putty in her hands, waiting for her to decide his fate.

$$* \qquad\qquad * \qquad\qquad *$$

Jessica awoke in the early hours of Saturday morning. After her visit to Miles she had slept fitfully, falling asleep over her book. She dreamt of running through the streets of London warning of the plague. People were wearing seventeenth century costumes, periwigs and crinolines and she was trying to fight her way between them. They ignored her. Beggars reached out to grab her hands and she ran away harder, afraid of disease. A young woman with long yellow hair offered to show her the way home, but she thought it was a trap and ran the other way. Miles appeared and laughed at her. She screamed at him and woke unsure whether she had really screamed out loud or not. It was six in the morning. The novel she had been reading was about the Plague of London.

She groped her way to the kitchen to make tea. The Oaf was away for a few nights on some geography field trip. He had asked her to keep an eye on his car parked in the street outside. She looked out and checked that it was there under the yellow street light; a shabby old car, but one he rated highly for some reason. She was making her way back to her room when she had the idea. There was the car and probably in his room somewhere were the car keys. She could drive up to Cumbria and tell her mother what had happened – the lunch she had spoiled, the row with Miles, the presence of Sue in Miles's flat – and be back before the Oaf knew she had gone. Did she have her driving licence with her? Did she have enough money for petrol? If she left now, what time would she get there? Was there a map anywhere? She must look on the web for a map.

She rushed about turning over piles of clothes and files until she found her licence and her purse into which she slid her credit card. All right so far! She crept into the Oaf's bedroom. He had left it in a mess but, thankfully, the car keys were thrown on the unmade bed as if waiting for her to find them. Back in her room she switched on her computer, found her mother's address and typed it into Mapquest. She asked for a journey plan and printed pages came out taking her out of London right into Milnethwaite. It said the journey could take five hours. She looked at her watch. If she went now, it was already seven o'clock, she'd be there by lunch-time and could even get back the same day and have the car back before the Oaf returned should he come home early. She'd have to take her chance of getting it back into the same parking place but she'd think of something if she couldn't.

Fired up with energy, she dressed in jeans and a sweater, packed a few things, including an anorak - Mum said it rained all the time - locked her door and was soon out in the street fitting the key in the car door. "Mum ought to know what is going on," she said to herself as she drove off, the car choking and stuttering, until she reached the main road. She went through empty streets as the dawn skies eased up a curtain of dark night clouds to reveal a grey morning. She drove through the Blackwall tunnel onto the M 11, finding her way through waking London by stopping at regular intervals to look at the map. She was enjoying herself. Action, that is what she needed. She stopped at a motorway service station for petrol and there were flowers, cards and chocolates on sale for Mothers' Day. She chose a card and a box of Belgian chocolates, pleased that it would look as if she had planned the trip to coincide with Mothering Sunday. She switched on her mobile and locked the car door – remembering the advice to lock herself in if ever in the car alone - and drove off. Good old Oaf! Not a bad car!

She had never driven so far before. She kept noticing 'Tiredness Kills' signs, blinking her eyes to keep awake. When she began to see hills and moors, it was easier to stay awake because she was scared in case the car broke down in this huge expanse of empty land. She'd seen piles of something or other on the hard shoulder and someone in a yellow coat waved to her to stop but she didn't dare. After turning off left into the Lake District an occasional sweep of sunshine revealed an astonishingly beautiful landscape but mostly she was in awe of the miles and miles of the most frightening mountains she had ever seen. Gradually they gave way to more modest curves on the horizon as she turned off towards Milnethwaite. She passed a few red and white notices nailed onto five bar gates between the black winter hedges that enclosed the narrow roads.

" Not very beautiful now, is it!" she proclaimed aloud.
It was well into the afternoon when she eventually drove between grey houses into the village and stopped to ask the way from an old woman with a dog who directed her to the barn beside the church.

"You visiting the painter lady, Mrs Creed?" Alice asked.
"That's right."
"You'll find her there all right" - must be her daughter up for Mothering Sunday.

*　　　　　　　*　　　　　　　*

Alice had gone on walking Spot despite the restrictions. He had to get out despite the epidemic. She kept him on his lead and rubbed her shoes and his feet in the bucket of disinfectant every time she went past the lych gate. She was very upset about Eric when she heard the news. She had gone to school with Jim and his brother. No-one dared get the wrong side of them as they would win any fight going. She remembered the biggest fight ever in the village when they were all kids. Jim had won it when he was a lad. Jim took on big Frank who used to live up the lane by their farm. It was a terrible scrappy fight as if a bull had been taken on by a terrier. Jim was a wiry chap at the time and it was a triumph - like David and Goliath. Eric though was not that strong and she'd thought perhaps he might spare a thought for her when no-one else did, but being the younger son, he had to move out and rent a farm the other side of the county and he'd married a girl from Whitehaven and took her with him, leaving Jim to carry on the farm.

Jim and Eric were respected farmers, doing things the old

fashioned way like their Dad and Jim did well to marry Ethel who carried on like her mother-in-law. She came from a farming family up near the coast. The wedding was a fine do. Alice had been over with her friend to see them come out of the church and to catch a view of Eric in his best suit. Ethel was very respectable and once in Home Farm, she had quickly taken on running things in the village. Everybody knew that she had a hard job with Jim. Quick-tempered, like his dad who had frightened them all when they were kids. Not like Eric. Jonty's more like Eric, she thought, That's why she had such a soft spot for him and tried to keep him out of harm's way, especially from his Dad. She knew he was smitten with the painter lady. She'd seen his other romances come to nothing. She could have told him they would. He went for the wrong girls every time. And now with Eric committing suicide, it would further unsettle Jonty. Of course it would, poor young man. It unsettled her too for that matter. She had a weep about it, though nobody but her'd know why. Would they be able to bury him decently, she wondered, with all this going on?

Alice knew that folk thought she was the village gossip but there was nothing wrong in wanting to know what was going on. She'd had to live alone, except for her dog, whereas everyone else had someone or other to talk to. She had been watching the painter lady and Mrs Cornfew, as she now was. They'd made good friends, my word, they had. She shook her head in wonder as she thought about them. They were both very educated women. They would see eye to eye about things. She knew all about the Mrs Cornfrew. She had cleaned for her poor husband. She knew his first wife too, poor lady. He had been kind to her as he was to everyone in the village as well as to all his patients. She didn't hold it against any man that he took his comforts where he could find them. So she never criticised him when Mrs Cornfrew, now is, began to visit him. Old Alice knew but she never said nothing. Like in the bible. "She who casts the first stone."

*   *   *

Polly was just about to begin painting again after a late lunch break when the door burst open and through it exploded Jessica.

"My God!"

"Aren't you pleased to see me?"

"I'm astonished to see you. Whatever….?"

"I just wanted to see you."

Polly hugged her daughter with mixed reactions. How like Jessica! Whatever she wanted to do, she did. Jessica was excited by her success in breaking the bonds of her boring life to get her story to her mother before anyone else did. She had driven further on her own than ever before and the car had not packed up and she had not crashed into anybody or got herself hopelessly lost. She was in a state of triumph and presented the card and chocolates with great style and ceremony to a bemused Polly.

"But how did you get here?"

"I drove!" Jessica announced proudly.

"Dad's car?"

"Oh no. He doesn't know I'm here."

"Then whose, for goodness sake?"

"Does it matter? I'm here. Isn't that enough?"

This didn't stop Polly looking out of the window at the battered old car in the yard.

"Oh, all right," Jessica conceded, "It belongs to the bloke upstairs."

"That's generous of him."

"Well, actually he doesn't know."

"Jessica!"

"OK, OK! I know it was a bit cheeky and it means I have to go back tonight or early tomorrow morning, but I wanted to see you!"

She seized her mother by the waist and danced her around the room and then stood still to look around before she flopped into the easy chair.

"Nice place!" she declared approvingly, then immediately got up again to look at the painting on the easel.

"What is that?" she cried. "It's weird! It's amazing!"
Polly was trying to withstand the force of Jessica's all-encompassing enthusiasm.

"It's a pyre for disposing of animal carcasses."

"Oh yeah, it's that thing…..what's it called?"

"Foot and Mouth," Polly said drily.

"Oh My God! I forgot . I saw these terrible fires on the moors – Shap it was called. Now I come to think of it, they had places where you could clean your car tyres with disinfectant, I think it was, but I didn't stop. Oh My God! Should I even be here?"

" No. But as you are I'll find some food."

"Bacon sarny 'll do. Where's the loo?"
Jessica clattered excitedly up the wooden stairs while Polly went to the kitchen to prepare food. She heard Jessica pull the chain and then wander about above her. Polly chuckled at her daughter's impetuosity, until she saw her bouncing down the stairs, jumping the last few steps and holding aloft Tom's portrait.

"Who's this?" Jessica said, sitting down cheerfully in the easy chair and holding up the portrait.

"Someone I knew."

"Why knew? Why knew?

"He died."

"He's dead then?"

"Mm"

How long ago?"

"Last year."
There was a pause as the truth began to dawn on Jessica.

"You drew it, didn't you?"
Polly took a deep breath. As she placed Jessica's bacon sandwich and mug of tea beside her, she said quietly, "yes I did."

"Why by your bed then? Why was he so special?"
Polly could see the logic working itself out in her daughter's mind.

"Why, Mum? Why by your *bed*?"
Polly's brain spun fast trying to concoct a convincing explanation until her hesitation began to condemn her. She answered bleakly.

"I was having an affair with him when he was killed."
Jessica looked as if she had been slapped in the face.

"Did Dad know about it?

"No."

There was a pause while Polly watched Jessica's world crash before her eyes. She grieved that it was she who was forcing her daughter to encounter the facts of love and betrayal. Jessica then began a cross-examination slowly and deliberately, teetering on the edge of hysteria.

"How did he die?"

"In an accident".

"When exactly did he die?"

"Last November."

"Mum!" Jessica cried out with outrage and disbelief. "How *could* you!"

Polly sat down on the oak chair, leaning forward to prod the logs in the stove while she prepared herself to speak. But Jessica did not give her time because she jumped up and paced about the room in bewilderment, banging into the corners of tables and chairs, rucking up the mats, grabbing at cushions and flinging them down again to punctuate a tirade of condemnation.

"I came here to tell you about Miles's affair with a married woman who has a little boy," she screeched "and him thinking that it is perfectly all right to do that, when it isn't and I thought you'd care!" She paused as if for full dramatic effect. "And then you tell me that you had an affair yourself that only finished last November! I suppose it only stopped then because he went and died. Is that right? And you never told Dad about it. You deceived him by lying just as Miles' girlfriend lies to her husband and her little boy." She stood over Polly looking down on her with disdain and disbelief. "Didn't you care about the people who might get hurt?"

Piecing the story together relentlessly, she continued,

" And you ran away up here hoping that no-one would

find out. Is that it?"

"That is just about it, yes."

"So, if I hadn't turned up, I would never have known, is that right? And if I hadn't found out, Dad would never have known, is that right?"

"I hoped you would not need to know."

Jessica continued to pick up cushions and throw them down randomly until her energy suddenly ebbed away.

"Mum" she wailed again, throwing herself down on the sofa. "How could you!"

Polly did not know where or when or whether to start to recount the happenings of the last year and a half. She knew her words could stay forever in her daughter's memory. If she spoke carelessly or falsely or with any trace of self-pleading she would destroy any remaining trust in Jessica and Polly would lose yet more of her diminished self-respect. She had to believe in the authenticity of her love for Tom because her self-respect depended on it as did now her daughter's faith in her.

After more long minutes Jessica, sunk deep in the sofa, asked in a far away voice if she could go and lie on Polly's bed, adding for good measure, "unless there is anything else I will find there!" Polly preceded her upstairs, puffed up the pillows on her bed, pulled down the covers, got out a fresh towel, told her how the shower worked and then held out her arms to her, dropping them when Jessica didn't respond.

" Get some sleep," she said. "We'll talk more later if you wish".

She walked slowly downstairs. She heard Jessica shut the bedroom door behind her and throw herself heavily on the bed. She listened but heard no signs of distress. As a child, if she were upset, Jessica, much like Brian, would fall asleep before recovering. She picked up the portrait of Tom that Jessica had left beside her chair and moved it to the shelf behind the wood-burner. She crossed the room to the painting, briefly lit by the last slanting rays of winter sunshine. As the light began to fade, her fingers traced the faint image of Tom she had drawn in the foreground of the pyre. She then covered it over and went into the yard. The sky was darkening over the fells.

"Well, Tom," she said, "this is the beginning of the end." She walked out into the lane and set off on a short walk along the road out of the village to clear her head before Jessica reappeared.

*   *   *

When Jessica woke and went downstairs, Polly was no longer in the barn so she wandered about the room and put the kettle on to make herself tea. She caught sight of the portrait, now on the shelf, and picked it up again and looked hard at it. What had this man been like? The drawing was delicately done and the man was looking straight at her out of the frame. He was very good looking. And now he was dead. Was he worth her mother risking their family for? You could never tell from appearances what anyone was like but the portrait told her that her mother thought he had been worth it. She had driven up here in disgust with herself at the scenes she had created about Miles's affair over Sunday lunch and then at his flat. She had come to get comfort from her mother. Now, she had totally freaked out again, but this time with disgust at her *mother's* behaviour. She had a strong impulse to telephone her father immediately. He ought to know and she had the power to tell him. But the mature thing to do, she said to herself, would be to sit quietly and listen to her mother's explanation and then decide what to do next.

It was not long before her mother came back. She accepted a cup of tea from Jessica and they both sat down.

"Well?" said Jessica beginning the inquisition, " so, what did you see in him?"

"I met him through my work and he took an interest in it and eventually I agreed to go out to dinner with him and we fell in love."

"Just like that?" Jessica spoke with deep sarcasm, "That's all?"

Polly nodded.

"But what did you see in him?"

"Cleverness, confidence, charm, gentleness…."

"And he wanted you?" Jessica interrupted.

Polly nodded.

"And you wanted him."

"Yes," she said. "I'm afraid I did."

Jessica sighed, nonplussed, but impressed, in spite of herself, by her mother's daring. Polly told her that they had been lovers for about a year and then he was killed before either of them had decided what to do about it.

"You mean whether to finish with Dad."

"I had not faced up to that by the time he died".

"Have you now?"

Polly struggled to be truthful when she herself no longer knew the truth of this next part of her story. "No. That's partly why I am here…. and to get over his death."

Jessica nodded and continued to ask her questions. "Did he have a wife and family?"

"Yes, he was estranged from his wife and his daughters were away at school."

"So they had money"

"He was quite a wealthy man, yes."

"Not like Dad then"

"Jessica…." Polly said warningly.

"OK. You didn't do it for the money. I know, I know. But, Mum, why didn't being married to Dad stop you? "

Jessica was appealing to her for something beyond an explanation and Polly was well aware of how high the stakes were.

"All I can say is that Dad and I have been married a long time. We worked all the time, recently giving little time to each other. That is no excuse nor an adequate explanation but, no, marriage didn't stop me having an affair and I don't know whether it would have stopped if he hadn't died. I really don't know that."

"And now?"

"Jessica, I don't think I can tell you any more to enlighten you. I would if I could."

"Will you leave Dad?" Jessica's penultimate question was urgently asked.

"I came up here because I was shocked and very, very sad. I believed I had to be alone to face what had happened to me. I don't yet know what I ought to do. When I am sure what to do, I hope I shall be able to do it."

Now came the last question.

"Will you tell Dad now that I know?"

"I don't know."

Polly felt the enormity of the weight on them both of what each would now do. Only by saying what she believed to be true could she leave it to Jessica to decide for herself what to do.

And that is how it was left between them.

Polly made a meal and the rest of the evening, by the fire, Jessica talked about her own life as she had wanted so much to do - her fear that no-one would want her as she was neither beautiful nor clever, that she did not enjoy the course, was ashamed of herself for how she behaved towards Miles but that she'd enjoyed talking to Dad and listening to his problems, "like you used to, Mum."

At about 9 o'clock, Veronica telephoned. She had telephoned most nights since the Jonty episode. "I'm sorry it is so late so I won't keep you," she said. "I know you have your daughter with you for Mothers' Day".

"How on earth did you know that?"

"Alice! I just thought I'd check you were OK and to say I will wait to from you before I come for any more sittings, shall I?"

"I'm sorry, but yes, that is a good idea, thank you."

"Are things all right?"

"Goodness knows." said Polly, "I'll ring you soon."

By the end of the evening, it was at last possible for Polly to hug her daughter. Jessica was to leave in the morning to return the car.

Polly insisted that she was the one to sleep on the sofa because Jessica was driving the long journey back to London.

Settled with blankets on the sofa, she put out the light, remembering, with irony, that it was Mothering Sunday the following day.

Chapter Eight

On 26th March an army brigadier was appointed to take charge of the removal of slaughtered animals. 4 cases in Cumbria generated 1458 cattle and 17,270 sheep for slaughter.

Sunday, March 25th.

On Mothering Sunday, Ethel went to the early service in church. There was to be no service for the children. The visiting vicar had maintained one service in the week, cancelling all others to reduce the risk of spreading the virus. A band of faithful people had walked or driven to church throughout the epidemic, a journey allowed as long as they crossed no fields. Ethel slipped out quietly from home while the men were with the cows, carefully wiping her feet in the disinfectant. She had not been to church since the epidemic began.

Suicide was something to hide in normal times but now it had become a badge of the tragedy of the epidemic. Annie had told Ethel that there would have to be an inquest and this might delay the funeral, which, the police had said, might even have to wait until the epidemic was under control. As their school was closed, Annie's daughter had taken her children with her to stay with her mother and all were confined to the farm-house indefinitely.

Ethel knew she must go to church. Their lives were falling apart. She had to say prayers for Eric's soul and for Annie's state of mind and for her daughter and her young children. It was deeply shocking that he should do such a thing. She had to pray too for Jim and Jonty. To her great disappointment, once he had got over the immediate shock of Eric's suicide, Jim had resumed his surly attitude to Jonty. She was afraid for Jim's state of mind and health. He could very well get depressed like his brother and do something stupid or his blood pressure could rise and produce a stroke. If the Foot and Mouth reached them this week they would be in no state to confront it. She needed to pray for them all, herself included.

The church was quiet. There were no flowers. The flower rota, for the first time in her life, had been suspended. It was more like war-time. The day was clear and the fells were bright with pinks and greys and the sky blue with scudding clouds. How she longed for colour and sunshine. She loved the village in the spring and today the church should have been full of spring flowers and she would have made bunches for the children to give their mothers - snowdrops and green-sheathed daffodils padded out with sprigs of pink flowering currant blossom. She went to her usual pew and, after nodding good morning to the few regulars, including Alice, knelt down. She wanted some peace. She had come to this village as a newly married woman. She had always loved the church and brought young Jonty to be christened and as a little boy to Mothering Sunday to collect flowers for her.

She had thought she might have grandchildren to bring here but Jonty seemed unlikely to marry now. He'd had a few tries that had come to nothing. She thought that a lass he met from Lancaster was going to turn out all right but then it'd come to an end and Jonty wouldn't talk about it. And now all the likely girls had married or gone away and he was now well over thirty. She felt sore that Jim was so hard on him especially as Jonty had given up any chance of moving out of the village or doing anything else with his life in order to help his father. Many sons would have walked away. She feared that he stayed for her sake. Jim was a harsh man, just like his father who took it for granted that a son's place was with his father and both of his sons had done just that and now Eric was gone. Other sons with the prospect of their fathers going on farming into their seventies, read the signs of the times and went off to work in garages, as the NFU men had warned. Jim chose to ignore the fact that his son was capable and ready to take on the farm now. Jim's lungs were in a poor way and she worried about his heart too. In shock he'd said he'd hand the farm over but doubted Jonty would take it on. At the year-end, Jonty had wanted to take sheep off the fells but Jim would have none of it. Since the epidemic he'd been in an awful state, persisting in keeping things as they always had been, which they were not, and only taking note of Jonty's information from the websites to dismiss it. Though he'd no more answers to the present crisis than anyone else, he behaved as if everyone were a fool but him.

However, Eric's death had galvanised him in a strange way. He was going about his work with an almost holy dedication. His decision to stick by the rules and not pay respects to his brother's body or to look to his widow had been part of a renewed resolution to protect his herd. It was the family herd they had built up over years. That was the sort of farming they thought was right, how they had always done things – not the so called 'flying herds' of those young men who bought and sold without loyalty to their own stock.

Her reverie was interrupted by the vicar coming in from the vestry. At this early service he used the old comforting words. 'The manifold sins and wickednesses which we from time to time most grievously have committed by thought, word and deed,' they all repeated. Well, it had been deed as well as thought and words with Eric all right and Jim and Jonty had come to blows. The house was bogged down in it all. Resentment was like mud stuck to their boots and never dug out at the end of the day. For her part she went round dusting and polishing as if she could flick away the layers of unhappiness that had settled everywhere. So, though the two of them were not in church, never were, except at Harvest and Easter, she would say "Sorry" for them. And she prayed for the soul of Eric, for Annie and her family and for Jim and Jonty, that the epidemic would pass them by. She prayed for the children in the village missing Mothering Sunday and not playing football in the field nor jumping over the nettles nor sloshing through the streams. She prayed for all the calves and cows and sheep that were slaughtered and piled up waiting to be buried or burnt. And for herself that she would have the strength to keep her good sense and that they would get through this ordeal somehow without losing all their stock and any of them getting ill or going mad or worse.

Then the vicar preached a short sermon, quoting the

Bishop who had written that the 'harmony of God's creation is ruptured', she thought he said. He said that 'sharing pain was best without words' but done in kindness. He talked of the telephone networks that were supporting people. She thought of herself ringing her sister-in-law every Sunday night and now ringing Polly Creed who was being very kind and understanding and who was a good woman, no matter what Alice kept hinting about with Jonty.

As she left the church porch and walked into the sunshine, the vicar gave her a warm hand-shake that made her feel that there was some help somewhere even if he wasn't their proper vicar. No vicar'd be able to do anything about Jim anyway although the old vicar would have tried. He was a hard nut for anyone to crack. On the way home she decided that she would have to say something to him, warn him about his health cracking up if he kept on beating himself up with work and worry and turning on Jonty the way he did, never mind her.

"Morning Alice," she said firmly, as she left the church porch to walk back home. If Alice had it in mind to add anything to the store of gossip about her family, Ethel would not be giving her the chance.

"Morning Ethel. Sad no Mothering Sunday flowers"

"It is, " said Ethel as she walked up the path, "very sad."

"And very sad about Jim's brother. Who'd have thought it?"

"Who indeed Alice. These are terrible times."

"I expect they'll keep the funeral until it is all over," Alice said.

"That's what our Annie's been told," said Ethel giving nothing away.

"Well, all these restrictions didn't stop Mrs Creed's daughter driving up to see her mother for Mothering Sunday."

"How did you find that out, Alice?"

"She asked me the way, didn't she. Must have been her. Nice looking girl. Not a bit like the mother mind you. Not so good looking, if you ask me."

"Now Alice," Ethel said firmly, "it's good that Mrs

Creed's got a daughter who cares enough to come all this way to see her on Mothering Sunday."

"That's what I thought," said Alice," and young Jonty ….well he's a fellow. Not one for Mothering Sunday, I bet."

"That's right" said Ethel getting to the top of the path and setting off fast in the opposite direction.

Sunday lunch was a silent affair in the farm kitchen. They listened to the lunchtime news on the television in the kitchen to avoid talking. It confirmed what Jonty had seen on the computer earlier in the day. He repeated the numbers.

"4 cases in Cumbria had generated 1458 cattle and 17,270 sheep for slaughter with delays for culling of up to 96 hours."
Jim muttered at the incompetence of the operation while Ethel tried to silence him by saying that Sunday was a day of peace. At the end of a tense meal, Jonty helped Ethel clear the table and Jim stumped off to bed for his customary Sunday nap. Before he left the room Ethel summoned up her courage to speak.

"I want to talk seriously to you both. Meet me in the living room after I've finished the dishes. At three o'clock sharp." Turning to her husband she said, " I'll set the alarm and wake you up."

Both men grumped off to their bedrooms. Jonty was alarmed by his mother's intended speech for quite other reasons than those preoccupying Ethel. Had Polly said anything to his mother about him? There had been no reply to his note – not that he should expect one. The upset about his uncle might have put it out of her mind until now and that was why she was calling this unusual family meeting. Or maybe, Alice had spoken about it to her this morning at church. She found out about everything in time. He stood staring out of the bedroom window thinking what would happen if people found out what he had done. Then he caught sight of Polly coming out of the yard and walking up the lane. She had her head down and he thought she looked sad. He watched her until she went out of sight, in agitation at the sheer sight of her again. He stayed glued to the window until she reappeared and went back into the barn. He then threw himself on his bed, imagining a number of different scenarios. How different from his previous imaginings about her! She would have read his note but what would she do about it? At the very least, he was sure she would never speak to him again. At worst, he daren't think.

At three o'clock, all three met up in a strangely formal way in the living room. Both men sat awkwardly turned away from each other. Ethel had decided to conduct the occasion like a Mothers' Union meeting so she sat upright and lifted her shoulders and cleared her throat before she began.

"Now I've asked you to come and listen to me for a change because I'm very worried." She looked at them both sitting like she imagined reluctant soldiers would at a briefing and marvelled at her courage.

"We've all had a terrible shock," she said, "and on top of that we learn this week the foot and mouth might get as far as here. Am I right?"

"Right enough," agreed Jonty. Jim sniffed.

"Well, if it does and even if we're lucky, God willing, and we don't get it, we'll likely lose our cows and calves through this continuous cull thing. Am I right? Now we've just got to pull together is what I want to say to you and I'll not put up any longer with this squabbling between the two of you."

Jonty began to feel relief. Was that all that was coming? Jim looked as if he'd be leaving any minute.

"These are hard times," Ethel went on, sensing that Jim would not listen much longer, "so, Jonty, you've got to work with your dad without pulling faces and grumbling. You're a man and you've got to act like one."

Jonty said meekly, "You're right, Mum." He was now in a state of mind to agree to almost anything.

"And Jim. You've got to let Jonty help you more. He's got to be given a chance."

"He's got that bloody computer, hasn't he?" said Jim in his usual tone of self-defense.

"That's not what I mean. I mean with the thinking as well

as with the doing. If we get this dreadful thing there's a lot of bearing up and hard thinking to do both now and into the future."

"Don't you think I know that woman?"

"There you go, Jim," said Ethel keeping going, "snapping at me when I'm just speaking a few words to you." Jim harrumphed. "You know what the doctor said about your blood pressure and that. Just be careful, is all I'm saying. I don't want anything to happen to us as has happened to poor Eric and Annie. There! I've said it. If this foot and mouth comes then we have to pull together."

"Is that the end of the lecture then missus?" said Jim making to get up.

"It is except to say that we have all three to get over Eric's death whichever way we can. That's all of it. You can go to the milking now but mind you're civil to one another."

She got up and left the room and, taking a deep breath when she was outside the door, she went straight upstairs to the bedroom. Jim left the living room first, followed by Jonty who was unintentionally grinning slightly as he passed him.

"What you grinning for?" Jim suspected that he was laughing at him for being told off by his wife like a child.

"Nothing," he said hiding his relief, "let's get to the sheds Dad, shall us?"

*   *   *

Jessica drove off after breakfast and Polly went into the barn in a very unsettled state of mind. It had been an extraordinary week. In addition to the pyre and Jonty, Ethel had told her of Jim's brother's suicide. These were events beyond her control getting tangled with things that were down to her. In heavy black lines, she drew a cartoon of herself struggling to be free from it all.

It had not been enough to run away, however cleverly she had contrived it. Her determination not to get involved with people in the village had crumbled under the pressures of the crisis and when Ethel agreed to her putting a telephone into the barn she had taken no account of the impact of family calls. Jessica stumbling on the truth about Tom had shaken them both. She had virtually lied to Miles. Brian would soon telephone and she would have to talk about the crisis here without mentioning the crisis waiting to erupt between them. Finally, even though she had begun to paint what she had seen on the moor and was excited by what was taking shape on the canvas, she knew she had not, anyway near, reached the core of the painting.

*   *   *

Jessica had arrived back early on Sunday afternoon to find that the Oaf's parking space was taken. She reversed noisily and parked the car untidily around the corner. The rest of the day, while snacking food, tidying the mess in her room and doing her washing, she kept an eye on the space hoping one of the cars would be collected so that she could move the car back to its rightful place. At last a gap appeared but by the time she had fetched the car and driven back to the space, it was already taken. By then, of course, the space she had left had gone! She could see no end to this circus so, in utter despondency with herself and the world, she drove the car round and round the streets before she could park it, concocting ever more crazy explanations about why it was not where it should be. She remembered her mother once saying "You can't improve on the truth". And here was her mother having lived a lie and she never knew.

She forced herself to go to College and agreed to join a group to go clubbing which she normally declined to do. But when there, she drank liberally into the early hours in an effort to lose her usual inhibitions. Rick, a guy from her class, commandeered her to dance and at three o' clock the whole group surged out noisily onto the pavement. It was too late to take a tube home so with Rick and others, she crowded into a car, to end up preparing to sleep on the floor of a flat in Clapham. She unambiguously encouraged him to believe that sex was to follow and they ended up on a mattress on the floor undressing at once in a drunken fashion. Having sex with him, with anyone, might cancel out, pay off, her mother's affair. Why not. From now on, she would do just as she pleased, where and when she pleased and with whom she pleased. Rick on cue, tussled with her, fumbling in his inexperience. She meant to help him to get the whole thing over quickly but when it was far advanced she suddenly heaved herself up from under him in a wave of deep distaste. He fought to continue and swore loudly as she pulled away, grabbed her clothes and stumbled over his legs into the bathroom. There she sat shivering, pulling her flimsy shirt around her and struggling into her jeans. She stayed there, huddled against the door until it began to get light. Then she crept back into the room to get her coat, looking down on him as he slept in a tangle of blankets. A narrow escape! He was only a shade better looking than the Oaf and she was disgusted at what she might have done. She caught an early tube that was almost empty and clanged the whole journey, before walking back to her room in the dawn. There she found a note on her door.

"Next time you use my car, ASK!"

*   *   *

Brian had restrained himself from ringing Polly before Sunday despite his eagerness to tell her of his latest visit to Tom's widow. He feared Polly would accuse him of glorying in Tom's misfortune. He also thought of telling her about how he had bested McNally but Polly would think that childish too. So he rang as usual soon after six o'clock. She snatched at the phone, thinking it was Jessica. She had seen her drive off, anxious for her safety.

"How's the work?" Brian enquired in a friendly tone.

"I'm very busy," she replied.

"What doing?"

"A large painting of something I saw."

"Good, good," he said, not asking for more details as he

knew she often wouldn't talk about a painting until she'd finished it.

"And how are things up there? Not got it yet have you?"

"No, but the brother of the farmer here committed suicide a few days ago on account of his animals being slaughtered."

"That's terrible, Polly. How simply terrible."

"And you?" she asked quickly to avoid a discussion about the epidemic.

"I've had a most interesting week!"

"That's good."

"Two interesting things in fact."

"Tell me."

"The most important is the departmental syllabus review being conducted by Ron McNally. I mentioned it to you?"

"Did you? Oh yes, perhaps you did."

"Well I now think I can make it useful."

"I might have guessed that you would dread it."

"I suppose I did… but McNally, you recall him, has proved to be rather inexperienced and I think I can actually help him."

"Good. That's good. You sound a bit more cheerful."

"Yes I do as a matter of fact."

"And the other thing?"

"It's about Tom Frost."

Polly was immediately in suspense.

"You'd never guess," Brian continued "but he is suspected of having spent, lost, concealed or even defrauded the College of more than half a million." He paused for a shocked response. There was none.

"Are you there, Polly?"

"Yes" she replied. "I'm here."

Her stomach seemed to dissolve. It was as if her body had registered the severity of the shock before her mind was able to do so, like some cartoon character overshooting a cliff edge and continuing to run madly before crashing into the sea.

"I thought you'd got cut off or something," Brian said. "Well, you won't credit it, but the VC asked me to visit his widow again - Marjorie is her name - I may have told you that - to see if I could find out his solicitor's name and address as they want to pursue this thing quietly before getting any formal investigation under way."

"So you've been to see her again?"

"Yes, I went on Friday."

He slowed himself down. He realised that he was enjoying telling her the news of Tom's fall from grace.

"Not only has this come to light, Polly, but Marjorie, Mrs Frost that is, has found out that he owned properties she had known nothing about – in London, in New York and maybe elsewhere and at least the one in New York he left to some woman. 'His mistress,' Marjorie called her. Apparently Tom had been having affairs for years with other women. A serial womaniser, it seems."

The barn was now totally dark except for the light from the fire.

"Polly, are you there?" Brian said, hearing no response "What do you think of that?"

"I don't know what to think," she managed to say.

Brian went on excitedly with his story. He told her that Tom and his wife were estranged and that she had lost track of what he did with his time and money and was now getting a stream of unwelcome information. He couldn't think how she must feel being deceived like that and he only hoped Tom had left her well provided for and that she didn't become liable for the debts or corrupt transactions he may have left behind him.

"Imagine," he concluded, "he, a financial guru, and there he is dying and leaving a mess behind him for others to clear up. Of course, there may be quite reasonable explanations, as I said to the V.C., but it certainly reveals a Tom I didn't recognise. I wonder if the man had had a breakdown. Then as an afterthought he added, "mind you, there are probably some very uncomfortable people around now waiting for the truth to come out."

Polly knew she must end the call at once so she told Brian that there was someone at the door.

"What on a Sunday night?" he said.

She lied that it was Ethel. She'd ring him back later. He told her not to bother – he just wanted to pass on the news to her as he'd told no-one else and was going to tell the VC the full story in the morning.

"I'll ring you to tell you how I get on, shall I?"

"Do, if you wish," she said. "Goodnight Brian" and put the phone down.

She sank into the easy chair, head in hands, to stem a wave of fainting. Her mind sped through a wild range of thoughts. What about the flat he had bought for the two of them? If he had left a property to another woman would he have left the London flat to her? Surely he would not be so unwise. And had he still been involved with this woman in New York at the same time as with her? He had travelled to a University there several times while they'd been together. Then Brian implied that there were other affairs. When were these other affairs? Did he have other women elsewhere in his life while he was with her?

She was by now in a state of agitation, getting up, walking around, drawing the curtains, sitting down, even clutching cushions as Jessica had done hours before. Terrible doubts were flooding into her mind. Did he use this so-called "estrangement" from his wife as a carte blanche to a clutch of affairs? Was she, Polly, one among many? Was this great love of her life just one in a row for him, or, worse, even one in a collection? A wife in every port? Must she believe what she had heard? After all, she knew Tom, whereas Brian's account was all hearsay. Coming from Tom's widow, from whom he was estranged, it could well be exaggerated and vengeful. On the other hand, the Vice-Chancellor would scarcely have been misinformed about the financial questions. Could she believe one half of the jigsaw and not the other? If he had been alive she would have demanded to know the truth. And, she thought ruefully, she would have believed his reply. Would she now?

She began once more to retrace the affair, from its beginnings to the first time he had made love to her and then to the routine of the secret assignments until his death. But this time she was going over it with suspicion. He had searched her out. Was this because he was looking for a likely woman? She had rebuffed him, but, detecting, somehow maybe, that she had switched off her sexual life, he had cleverly awoken it. How? She knew how. Then he had acted quickly to "bed" her by making a speedy arrangement with a friend. But had he used this friend's flat before with other women? When he had succeeded in taking apart all her defences, one by one, he had been able to buy the flat in a matter of days or weeks. Where did that money come from? Where did that leave her? She had never had an affair before, nor believed she ever could. She had never questioned whether that was the same for him. If he hadn't actually deceived her, he had not told her the truth either. If this woman in New York existed, was she in the same category as herself, set up with a place to share with him. Now that she couldn't demand an explanation from him, she was left high and dry, descending into a spiral of disillusion at his deceit. He had never loved her.

That night was as sleepless as the very first ones in the barn. She dreamt of Tom appearing and disappearing. She was searching for him when he was gone and striking out at him whenever she found him. Her mind was wrestling with an entirely new picture of him. She sat up in bed, put the light on and looked at her drawing of him where she had placed it again at her bedside when Jessica had left. Was she a fool?

Why didn't she know about his background? He said it was conventional and of no interest. He came from somewhere in the Midlands, he'd said. He went to university in Sheffield where he met his wife. Beyond these facts she knew little. His career, he said, had been built on his intellectual and entrepreneurial ability but was deficient in art and musical knowledge, which is why she had accepted the notion that he wanted to learn from her? Was this all a pretext for sex? She thought of politicians whose adrenalin pumped so hard that they conducted affairs seemingly in order to keep it high. They took foolish risks, living dangerously in the belief that they could get away with anything.

"My God, Tom! Was that you?" she moaned. "Was that you?"

*   *   *

At breakfast, on Monday, despite Ethel banning all news at breakfast-time, Jonty shouted into the kitchen from the computer that it had been confirmed on the Food and Drink Federation website, that a brigadier had been appointed to co-ordinate the management of culling and disposing of animals. Jim's depression made way for a flicker of satisfaction.

"I told you," he growled. "I told you they needed the army. "
It had been announced a week before that military commanders would be appointed for Cumbria and Devon to take over the whole logistical operation. It had been the day the Prime Minister had been in the county, addressing an angry crowd of Cumbrian farmers. The most informative website that Jonty had discovered, had said that the Prime Minister had been impressive. He had promised to get the movement of culled stock speeded up. The brigadier had listened to their complaints and criticisms and actually said that the farmers themselves and local hauliers and contractors could have handled the crisis better than the ministry. Jim was deeply pleased at this.

Jonty went on to explain that a standard tariff would be applied to reduce delays in slaughtering cattle instead of farmers having to wait for vets to value every herd.

"Too bloody late!" cried Jim.

*   *   *

On Monday morning, Polly forced herself to get in the car and drive to town. Shopping took her longer than usual because she couldn't keep her mind focussed on the list and so repeatedly retraced her tracks around the shelves. She didn't speak to the woman on the till and then left her credit card on the counter so that someone had to run and fetch her back. She drove back to Milnethwaite in a haze and reached her door before remembering that she had to deliver the parcels to the farm. In turning the car around in the yard she scraped more paint off its wing and swore loudly, looking round to check that Alice was not on the lookout.

She telephoned Veronica to ask her to come round. She couldn't paint in this state and only had another three weeks of her sabbatical left.

"This afternoon?" Veronica asked, "Is it to continue with the portrait in which case I must wear the same clothes?"

"No, not the portrait. I just need to talk."

"Is it Jonty again?"

"No. I just need to talk to someone." She had forgotten Jonty.

Veronica arrived that afternoon and Polly was ready to open the door as soon as she heard the car draw up. She explained rapidly what Brian had told her about Tom's financial discrepancies, the bequest of the flat in New York to another woman and the story of Tom having many other women. As Polly talked, Veronica tried to make sense of the story, weighing it with the effect of Jonty's visit. When she raised this Polly dismissed it because Jonty had apologised! It was clear that this information from her husband called into question the whole point of her visit to Cumbria.

"He never loved me," Polly concluded. "I was duped."

"You've had far too many shocks too close together."

"All of my own making," wailed Polly.

"I don't think so." Veronica said. "Why do you say that?"

"I shouldn't have fallen for him."

"Can you be so sure this story is true?"

"If he were a 'serial womaniser' then it makes me a mere prey!" Polly bitterly spat out the words. "If having an affair was for him *habitual* when for me it was utterly exceptional, I was totally deceived. He deceived me!"

"Couldn't you trust rather to the truth of your own experience of him?"

Polly paused, weighing up her reply. "No. He seduced me!"

"What makes you so sure this was not love?"

Polly almost brayed her reply. "Because he was so bloody good at it!"

After a pause, Veronica asked, "does that make it bad?"

"If I was tricked" Polly wailed, "why did I not realise that?"

"You are being hard on yourself again."

"I am disgusted with myself as well as with him. It was all just sex"

There was a long pause as she began to sob.

This went on for a while – long enough, thought Veronica, to clear it out of her system. And then, no longer the counsellor, she took a risk. She folded her arms and looked straight at Polly, and said

"Is wanting sex so very terrible? I don't think so."

Veronica crazily recalled that she had once struck and stunned a goose about to attack her and the goose had stopped in its tracks, totally dizzied. She watched a similar effect on Polly. She stopped sobbing and looked at Veronica in disbelief. Then, suddenly Polly put back her head and laughed. Pent up tension exploded not in tears but in gusts of laughter. Veronica sat with her hands clasped in front of her, smiling uncertainly. She must have sounded as if she approved of affairs. In her own case she supposed she had. She even began to laugh a little herself.

At last, pulling herself upright Polly spoke.

"I should have asked him more questions."

"To which you may never now know the answers," said Veronica.

"I may never know the answers about him, but inside," Polly replied, feeling very sure of her ground, "I know the answer about myself. I fell for him because I needed something to change and he offered a short cut. I *may* not have been a total fool and he *may* not have been a total swine," she sighed," but I now know that he would not have been the answer for me, even if he had lived, and I think I knew even then."

"Good," said Veronica. "That sounds better. She made a cup of tea, as Polly stood up and walked around. "You now look absolutely exhausted. After this tea, will you come and stay the night *this* time?"

Polly smiled and shook her head, "I shall be all right now. Thanks."

"Sure?"

"Oh Yes." And then "How old are you? I have never asked."

"Eighty one."

Polly shook her head. "But I thought….."

"You thought age went with certain views? I remember the war and the fact that those left alive learnt a lot about human nature."

*   *   *

Veronica drove away with a date for resuming the portrait and Polly went for a walk to clear her head. During the evening and into the night she set about reconstructing every stage in the affair. She needed to get it in order in her mind now that the story was so changed. On the one hand, his courtship was debased to seduction and his love-making to sexual performance and then, as if a vinyl record were flipped over to the other side, she would force herself to look to see if she could recover any tender memories to assess whether any of them could have been genuine on his part.

In the end she saw clearly as never before that Tom's betrayal of her was equalled by her betrayal of Brian. She recalled the many lies she had told him with deep discomfort. Before settling down to sleep, she took the drawing of Tom that she had returned to her bedside after Jessica's visit, and put it firmly in the drawer, leaving the photograph of Brian, Miles and Jessica.

Chapter Nine

On 29th March a Vaccination Seminar was held at 10 Downing Street, chaired by the Prime Minister and attended by the Minister of Agriculture, the Chief Veterinary Officer, the Chief Scientific Adviser, Government and non-government scientists.

The last days of March.

After his call to Polly the previous night, Brian began the day purposefully. He made an appointment with Vice-Chancellor. He had a good story to tell and could imagine the VC's reactions, man to man, to the intricacies of Tom's private life. But when later in the day, he entered the great man's study by appointment, his intentions had changed. He had liked Tom. Should you gratuitously demolish a colleague's reputation if he had treated you as a friend, simply because you could? The Vice Chancellor did not actually need to know about how Marjorie was treated by her husband, leastways, not from him. So he merely handed the details about the solicitor over to him, said his widow was thinking of moving up north to be nearer to her children's school and that she had asked that the College deal in future only with her solicitor.

"Quite, quite," the Vice Chancellor replied. "Of course, of course. Thank you Brian." He took a deep breath and asked Brian to sit down.

"I'm going to make an exception to my rule of confidentiality and tell you more of what is happening, Brian, because, frankly, I need your opinion on one or two things.

"Certainly," said Brian full of misgiving, "if I can be any help….".

"I'm afraid we are learning more worrying facts about Tom Frost. He seems to have been borrowing from Peter to pay Paul and his research fund was Peter, so to speak, administered, one might almost say laundered, through the College. People are coming out of the woodwork with whom he, in our name, had contracted, on College notepaper, with his personal signature as

Professor. They are saying in writing – clearly they are talking to each other - that they had already given notice to their present employers and therefore consider they should be employed by the College to work in the Department while awaiting the appointment of a new professor. The Finance Department then tell me that, if they were to be employed, even on short-term contracts, there is insufficient money in the departmental budget to pay them, let alone money in the account. Even if we could get away with not employing them - and it is perfectly clear to me that we should not so employ them – we cannot simply pay them compensation either if it were proved that we were liable on the strength of Tom's cursed letters."

"Where has all the million gone that Tom raised?" Brian asked, having noted in passing that the V.C. was clearly committed to scrapping Tom's professorship.

The Vice-Chancellor sighed deeply. " Most of it is spent! It appears that there are large bills paid by the College under the research budget - which was very loosely worded by the way – you know, very fudgy budget heads – I don't know what the finance chaps were thinking of at the time. The fund is empty in real terms."

"But how on earth…?' Brian was totally bemused

"Well, for a start, there is a building in New York apparently intended as a research outpost connected to one of the big finance companies that is currently getting egg on its face after the collapse of some of the dot-com investments".

"But how was that approved?"

"I can only think that others, including Terry - who is very embarrassed, I need not say - were so much in awe of Tom, with his huge public profile, that they simply didn't ask the right questions when they signed the cheques!"

"That is incredible."

"If only it were not credible! Not quite as bad, but bad enough, there is a sizeable deposit paid on a flat in Central London and a mortgage commitment made."

"What's that for?" asked Brian.

"Don't ask me!" said the Vice-Chancellor in despair "Perhaps to house his mistress? How should I know!"

"Perhaps for him to stay after his late night broadcasts?" Brian was trying hard to rescue some belief in his one-time friend.

"Whether the mess would have been sorted out by him over time is possible, I suppose, but now highly in doubt; and, regardless of how he might have attempted to do that, with his skills, as we thought, of high-powered money-management, or should I say money-movement, what he did seems quite likely to have been fraudulent. This is all in the context of several trillion dollars having been wiped from the market value of some of the dot.com businesses that have gone bust and he was tied up with one of them. Some of the Board members have been convicted of misleading investors.

"Good gracious."

"Quite. Whatever comes of this, one thing is absolutely certain, even if we manage to re-coup some of the money, we shall be paying the most enormous legal fees! For which, I need not add, there is *no budget!*"

Brian was dumbfounded and taken aback by the VC's fury.

"And," the Vice-Chancellor added as a desperate after-thought, " all this is down to *me* for approaching him in the first place! On copper-bottomed recommendations, I might add in my own defence."

He paused, exhausted, leaving Brian flummoxed as he tried to think out how such a thing could ever have been achieved when the finance department was on *his* back all the time after their pound of flesh.

"I must say I thought he was a good chap. What did you make of the man, Brian?"

Brian said weakly, "I liked him and….. I believed in him."

"Quite," The Vice-Chancellor said emphatically. "So did we all."

"But he must have known this would come out."

"I confess to you, Brian - and this is what I really wanted

to confide in you - I have begun to wonder whether he took his own life, realising that the game was up and that his reputation would be in tatters. Because you know his poor wife and were a friend of his, could I be right to think that, do you suppose?"

"But there's been an inquest hasn't there? I understood it was an accident."

"Yes, yes, but could that not have been misjudged? Did his wife give you any hint that he was depressed?"

Brian did not know how to respond. He could, if he had to, tell him about Tom's womanising – that might well explain some of the property in some bizarre way, but he could say nothing about Tom's state of mind.

"Well, that is not our business of course," The Vice-Chancellor continued, "It's idle speculation and doesn't alter the facts. I can imagine what a time the Senior Common Room would have with this. But I would be interested in what you knew about the man though, you know, outside work."

Brian stuck to his resolution to say only what he knew, with the added dimension of caution that he might be asked by someone or other to give evidence if he was now being elevated to Tom's close friend.

"I know nothing of his other interests other than that he liked paintings and, for example, bought one of Polly's. He was a good support to me in meetings and I liked him. I thought of him as a breath of fresh air as he always focused on what was to be done. He never got bogged down in details."

"Perhaps," said the Vice Chancellor, with heavy irony, "he should have paid a bit more attention to details, eh? How is Polly by the way?"

"Painting hard I gather. Back in a few weeks."

The interview was over. Brian had succeeded in not betraying Marjorie's confidences. The College solicitors would talk about it with Tom's legal representatives and he need not be involved. However, he remembered that she had said previously something about Tom having more money than sense. He was now bound not to talk to anyone else but he wanted to talk to

Polly who had said something similar but she had been abrupt and pre-occupied the previous evening. He hated it when she cut him off in conversation as she so often had in recent times. It fuelled his fear that she might not actually come back to him. She had met so many people in her new job that, recently, in the early hours of the mornings, he had started to dread that there was someone else.

*　　　　　　*　　　　　　*

Sue at last rang Miles one evening.

"I thought I'd give you a ring to say sorry I haven't been touch and sorry about the train but I needed time to think and can we meet tomorrow evening and go for a meal?"

"Of course. I'll meet you after work."

"Great, Thanks. Gotta go"

"I love you Sue," he said, not sure she heard him before the phone went dead.

They met at an Italian restaurant in Bloomsbury. The waiter knew them from earlier visits and was solicitous in lighting a candle for them at their table. They ordered, asking polite questions about each other's health and work until the first course arrived. They then ate in silence until Sue began to talk.

"Firstly, I am very sorry that I ran off. It was unfair of me but I suddenly felt bad about being there."

"Was it my sister's doing?"

"No, not really. It was the sheer fact of your family and my family that made me realise that we couldn't go on."

"But I thought…. I hoped…." Miles stopped eating. He guessed that by the time he had eaten the food in front of him, it would all be over.

"Miles. You have been really good to me and I am very grateful…"

"Grateful!" he repeated. The word was a mockery of the relationship he thought they had. "So I was a good stop-gap."

"Miles, I never pretended that it was a permanent

relationship. You knew that from the beginning."

"Did I?" Miles knew very well that she had never made a commitment to him unlike his to her. "I simply do not understand how you could have behaved as you did unless you loved me."

She shrugged uncomfortably, pushing her fork around the plate but eating little. "I guess I was lonely in London. I suppose I should not have begun it but once we had begun it was hard to stop. I'm sorry. It hurts me too."

"Really!" he said sarcastically.

"I'm very sorry."

"How do you think it makes me feel to be dispensable when it suits you. And I know this is because you only have two weeks left on your project."

They ordered coffee and drank it in silence.

"Shall we meet again?" Miles asked quietly. Sue said there was no point. They sat in silence while the plates were cleared, then rose, he paid the bill, hailed a taxi for her, watched her drive off and set off on the walk back to his flat. When he undressed for bed he found the bill for the evening's meal crumpled in his coat pocket. He straightened it out and, aware of creating a small melodrama for himself, placed it in his diary alongside his business card.

The following evening he rang his father and told him, "by the way," that they'd all be glad to know that the relationship had ended. He refused to listen to his father's condolences and told him that he'd better worry, not about him, but about Jessica who seemed to be going off the rails, behaving appallingly at his flat the other night.

*　　　　*　　　　*

Brian waited until the following Sunday before ringing Polly. They exchanged details of the weather and the epidemic and she told him there was to be an inquest into Jim Stewart's brother. Brian was impressed as he had read a short paragraph about farmer suicides in the Independent, not connecting them with Polly.

"And how is your work?" she asked.

"I said I would tell you about my visit to the Vice-Chancellor."

"You did, yes."

"I learnt so many more things about Tom Frost that I simply could not believe until I compared them with what his widow said about his womanising. I now have to believe that he may actually also have been defrauding the College. It is almost unbelievable, but he might even have been financing his sexual affairs from College funds, making down payments on properties in which to conduct them!"

"If true, that is shocking," Polly said quietly.

"The Vice-Chancellor even feared that he was in such a financially compromising state that he might have crashed the car on purpose."

This was such a deep shock that she gasped and trying to control her voice replied "but that is not very likely is it?"

"I said I thought not. I didn't tell him that Marjorie told me about the other women."

"Why not?

"I don't want to be the one to lend credence to that sort of story. You know how the Senior Common Room would thrive on it!"

Unable to tell Brian that this could hardly be true - and to give herself time to think whether it might be given what she had heard at the Inquest - she swiftly changed the subject. "And your review?"

"That's going along fine. I have finished my preparation."

"Good. I knew you would."

"Did you?"

"Your work is very good, Brian."

"By the way, Miles is worried about Jessica. She went to his flat and harassed him further about his relationship. Have you spoken to her?"

"Yes I have." Polly did not mention the trip to Cumbria. "You have been good to her, Brian. Is Miles all right?"

"Sue, the young woman, has finished with him and gone back to her family. He wouldn't talk about it. "

"It was only a question of time, I suppose."

Then Brian took his courage in both hands.

"Are you coming back?"

"I thought I would drive back on Easter Saturday once I have finished the big painting I am doing."

"Thank God."

"Did you think I might not?"

"I had wondered. I have worried that your sabbatical was a chance to get away from me."

"Not from you, Brian. Perhaps from myself."

*   *   *

"My God," she said aloud once she had put down the phone. Would he have wanted to kill himself? She had good memories of that last night together. Could she have been wrong? She could trust nothing now.

She had sometimes day-dreamed of what life would have been like if he had left his wife for her. He had said he had no love left for Marjorie, so might he have been on the point of asking her to leave Brian. She had fantasised about the affair continuing. Their relationship, she had dreamed, could have stabilised into an enriching experience taking them both to new heights of personal achievement. She had even thought of resigning her teaching post in order to paint full-time, hiring a studio in one of those large warehouses in South East London. Away from the College, she and Tom could carry on without pressure. She had tried to imagine telling Brian to his face that she was going to leave him. Or perhaps she would write a letter after she had gone. Either way, she would ask him to forgive her and say that they both needed a fresh start before their lives slipped away. People took such decisions, she would say. They both knew people who had taken them or been on the receiving end of them. Good friends. And they had survived. Some had said, "I wonder why I hadn't done it before!"

But now, she thought, what if she had left Brian and set up home with Tom and then had found out these things about him; that he had other women not only in his past but in his present. And had not told her. And what if she had gone on to learn that he was to be disgraced because of financial dishonesty? She might try to convince herself that, being a consummate professional, he was in the process of arranging the money appropriately but death had interrupted him. But her abiding thought, to which she returned again and again, was that she had never really known him.

Walking about the room, her mind turned to another unexplored aspect of the whole affair. Marjorie. If she felt *she* was no longer sure of Tom, what on earth would his wife be feeling. Although they had never met, they were now strangely drawn together by the weird stroke of fate that it was Brian who was getting to know her. She recalled Marjorie as she had seen her at the funeral and the inquest with her daughters. She now had the task of supporting the daughters as she too learnt of Tom's financial and sexual escapades. Of which she, Polly, was one, the latest perhaps. Perhaps his wife was inured to his deceptions as she had never left him. Polly had taken at face value what Tom had said about her, but perhaps their relationship was strong despite his unfaithfulness. In the past upper-class women coped with such things.

How had she never given much thought to Marjorie; not sympathetic thought, not woman to woman thought. Instead, she had been content to have an affair with another woman's husband because he said he no longer loved his wife. If passion begot callousness, then she had been callous and Tom had been callous too. And more than once, it seemed. She took pen to paper and began to draw his face and then cut it up like a jigsaw, laying it together with wide gaps between the pieces. A portrait made up of fragments that had come loose and now hung together solely through the links with others' lives, connected through him, but which he had carefully kept apart: herself, Brian, Marjorie, his children, her children, other women and their children, trusted business colleagues, colleagues in the College. Creating a web of secrets and the winner was the one who got away with most? But he had lost his life. If not by suicide - which she still doubted - but by an accident that could now look a lot like poetic justice.

*   *   *

It was still too soon to go to bed so she rang Miles in the light of what Brian had told her.

"I'm so sorry that Sue has gone, Miles. Dad told me."

"Of course there was no future in it. I can see that now."

"That probably doesn't make it any easier to accept."

"You're right. You see, Mum, I've never really loved anyone before."

"I realised that she was really important to you."

"I'm gutted." He paused. "Mum, did you love anyone before you met Dad?"

"No," she replied truthfully, adding "but love does not always come when it's straightforward."

"How do you mean?"

"I mean that at times attraction seems to be driven by forces beyond our control."

"You were lucky with Dad then."

Polly was on the brink of telling him the truth. Though it still felt deceitful to stay quiet, she knew at once that it was no longer relevant to his situation. Everything was now changed.

"The ending of a relationship,in whatever form it takes, is one of the most painful things in life," she said.

'You're right, Mum." At which she shook her head.

*   *   *

Jessica was awoken by her mobile. She scrambled around inside her bag and bleerily answered it. It was Miles.

"Where've you been these last few days. I've been ringing

you."

"To a club amongst other things"

"Didn't think you did them."

"I won't ever again!" she said defiantly. "It was awful. I made an ass of myself. So, what do you want?"

"To see if you are all right. And I thought I'd let you know that Sue has left me."

"Oh." She paused. "That's tough. I don't know what to say. Are you sorry?"

"Of course I'm bloody sorry!"

Then Jessica's mind did a somersault. "Oh God, you don't think….?"

"No Jess, it was not your fault. She's going back to her husband and son. I guess you were right all along."

"Oh Miles. I'm so sorry. I feel terrible. I mean I'm so sorry for all I said as she seemed very nice."

"She is, but it was not to be. Thought I'd let you know."

*   *   *

The next evening Brian rang Jessica and asked to meet her for a meal again. He attributed her reluctance to accept the invitation to her shame over her imagined contribution to the end of Miles's relationship. She, on the other hand, dreaded sitting across the table with him because the air between them would be full of her mother's secret, like a pall of cigarette smoke.

She had not given her word to her mother that she wouldn't tell him of the affair because her mother had said that when she had decided whether to tell him she would let Jessica know. Would she say that she had visited her? If she did, she would have to lie, not so much about why she had gone but about what had happened when she got there. Deceiving and lying had infiltrated the family. Miles had kept his affair secret until she found out, just as, until she found out, her mother had kept hers. She was caught in a trap.

They met in the same restaurant as before. Brian watched

his daughter as she came in. She was more trendily dressed this time, almost defiantly so. She also wore strange make-up as if adopting some obscurely tragic fashion.

"How are you darling?" he asked jumping up and holding out a chair for her.

"Fine thanks."

Her tone of voice was brittle.

"How's work? he asked, trying to sound more like a father than a teacher.

"So, so."

"We haven't seen each other since you came to Sunday lunch…"

"And spoilt it, I expect you are going to say?" she retorted.

"No" he said calmly, " I thought you were distressed and wondered how you are now."

"I'm fine," she said again and then, to distract him from a conversation that might lead her into lies or prohibited truths, she gave him her version of the visit to Miles; she had called to apologise, she said, but had done the opposite. She didn't know why!

"Sue seemed very nice, " she added.

Brian made no comment, trying to work out what was going on with her. So he asked her about her Easter plans and whether she was going to France.

"That was a crazy idea," she said. "I've made some new friends " - 'lie' she thought - " so I'll go to the wedding on my own, as some of my gang will be there too." Determined to avoid more questions she asked him about his work. He duly chatted away hoping that she might thereby relax. He told her in an upbeat manner that he was feeling 'chipper' and was using the McNally review to push through his own ideas about the department. He intended to make 'partnership with schools', a reality, he said, instead of the latest government buzz-word.

"You mean like 'choice' and 'blue water' and 'thinking outside of the box?"

"You've got it," he smiled. "As a matter of fact I've had

an interesting time recently with a buzz-character who used all those buzz-words - a Professor of "Business Studies," who made me feel stuffy and out of date. He was 'a mover and shaker.' But then he got himself killed."

Jessica looking fixedly at her father. "How did he die?" she asked in a level voice. She had asked her mother the same question.

"In a car accident," he continued, "and I was given the tricky task of visiting his widow."

"Why?"

"Oh, to return his belongings and ask for his solicitor's name and address. It was tricky because it seems he had been diddling the university."

"Why are you telling me this?" Jessica did not want to hear what he was telling her.

"Because it has made me realise," said her father, intent on telling his story, "that being smart doesn't always pay off; that there's a place for people like us who don't play around with money or women but stick to our jobs and our families."

"What's this about women?"

"Oh well," said Brian, not noticing the intensity of Jessica's interest, "he seems to have had a string of women into the bargain."

"Did you tell Mum all this?"

"Yes, when I phoned her on Sunday night. Your Mum knew him a little too of course."

Jessica thought her head would explode. She made a random excuse to leave but let her father drive her back.

As soon as she closed her door behind her, she leaned against it. "Oh my God". The secret was even bigger now. Her Dad didn't realise that the slimy bastard he described was probably his wife's lover! It simply had to be one and the same man! Again, she felt like breaking this secret open and letting the contents fly out like Pandora's box rather than be stuck with holding it all by herself.

She sat down on the bed, struck by the stark realisation

that the bottom line for her was that she must not let her parents separate. The family would be split forever and she would hate that. How could they stay together if her father found out that her mother had been unfaithful with a man he actually knew? A week ago she had believed passionately that her mother must tell him the truth. Now 'the truth' had become so contaminated, that any word or action of hers would lead to unforeseeable consequences. If she told Miles all she knew, he wouldn't believe her and would accuse her of wrecking other people's lives. If she told her father she would be acting as a sort of toxic virus in her parents' marriage, like this foot and mouth thing. She must either keep absolutely quiet or run far away.

Later in the evening, she decided to reassure her mother that she'd kept quiet.

"Mum. I have to talk to you," she said as soon as Polly picked up the phone. "I've just had supper with Dad and…"

"and…?" Polly said," you've…

"Before you think I have, I haven't told him."

"I see"

"No, you don't, Mum." She was almost shouting at Polly down the phone. "You mustn't tell him!"

"Jessica," Polly said "Calm down. Make sense."

"Mum, as that man is dead, you don't have to tell Dad you were having an affair with him!"

"Jess. Slow down!"

"Don't you see! You're finished with him. He's finished with you. It's over. You don't have to tell Dad."

"And what about lying? I thought that was so very important?"

"Mum, what's important is that you and Dad don't split up! That's what matters. If you tell him about this man, Dad will think you don't love *him* and he'll leave you or you'll leave him or something."

Jessica was desperately making the case without saying that she knew that this man, who must be her mother's dead lover, was a total shit!

"Jess…." Polly began.

"Mum, don't argue with me. I know I'm right. I'm sorry that this man of yours is dead, if you really liked him so much, but now that he's dead, it's a good thing in a way, so that he can't split up you and Dad. He hasn't the power any more. Dad loves you. I know he does. I love you both. *Please* mum, don't tell him. And by the way, Miles and Sue have finished and it wasn't my fault!"

Polly thanked Jessica for her call. In a soothing voice, she said she'd take into account what she'd said. Of course she didn't think that she'd broken up Miles's relationship. She thanked her for not telling her father and leaving Polly to do what she thought was right and at the right time, as they'd agreed. She repeated her promise that she would tell Jessica when she had decided what to do. Eventually she deemed Jessica calm enough to put down the phone.

*　　　　　*　　　　　*

When Brian got back from his meal with Jessica, there was an answer-phone message waiting for him. It was Marjorie Frost asking him to call. He dreaded getting further embroiled in Tom's affairs, so appalled was he at their extent. Marjorie's account married up with the Vice-Chancellor's but Brian was now caught between these two people's versions of apparently the same facts though neither was in a position to see, as he did, how Tom's bizarre, jigsaw-puzzle life might fit together - or rather had *not* fitted together. He began to wonder if Tom's had indeed come to pieces. Had a breakdown? Too many balls in the air? Had he taken his own life, knowing he was on the brink of discovery? Yet it was only his death that had exposed it all. How could he visit Marjorie knowing what he now knew? Nevertheless, the next morning he telephoned to fix a time to visit. In due course, there he was once more, driving through the open gates and sitting sipping tea in the same chair in the living room.

Marjorie, for her part, was not entirely sure why she wanted to see him again. He hadn't told her much. He didn't seem to know much. She could ask him if he knew anything more but she didn't really want to hear any more. The main reason she had asked him to come was that he seemed such a nice man; someone she could talk to. Unlike the solicitor and the bank manager who implied that there were a lot of things they were choosing not to tell her, Brian Creed seemed to have no ulterior motive. Her parents would help her decide about buying a house, her solicitor and bank manager would try to advise her about her money or lack of it, but the things she felt quite alone with were what Tom's death and dealings said about her and what to tell the girls about him.

For their sake, she had always tried to protect Tom's reputation. She kept up a façade about the vagaries of his life which she now desperately wanted to drop. Brian Creed seemed to be someone she could trust if she spoke as she really felt.

"I hope you don't mind my asking you to come again."

Brian shook his head and waited for the reason for his summons.

" I wanted to ask your advice."

The sat down and he still waited, fearful of what she was about to ask him.

"It's my daughters. I don't know what to say to them."

"About what?" he asked kindly and with some relief that it was not more personal.

"They worshipped their father you see. I kept from them everything that I knew would upset their view of him. They knew him as clever, generous, fun and devoted to them."

"Is there any need to destroy that image?" he asked gently.

"Well, from my point of view, knowing what I now know, it is a false image."

"Or an incomplete one perhaps. None of us knows everything about another person," Brian said tentatively. "I too thought Tom was a great person, though I hardly knew him."

"Precisely. He kept up this image but it wasn't true, was it?"

"But to his daughters?" Brian dodged giving an opinion

based on what he knew but she did not.

"He loved them of course, but…….." she hesitated .

"Was that false?" he ventured.

There was a long silence during which she began to cry quietly. Brian wondered whether to cross the room to comfort her, but stayed in his seat uncomfortably watching her. Unknown to him, she longed for him to come across and take her hand or give her a handkerchief or something. Just to be kind to her. She was longing, had been longing since Tom's death, for someone to comfort her. She had publicly kept up the pretence of Tom, the great man, much missed by all who knew him, but every time she was told of some other facet of his life, of his dishonesty, she felt ever more destroyed.

"It must be very hard for you to be learning all these things." Brian said uncertainly.

"It is terrible, terrible…. and terrible that I actually believe it all."

Her crying was so quiet, so achingly quiet, that he could no longer stay in his seat. He rose to go to her, offering her a handkerchief and kneeling beside her and taking her hand. She took the handkerchief, smiled gratefully and as the crying slowly lessened, put her hand on his. They stayed like that for a while.

This was not a role he had experienced before. Students failing teaching practice or Jessica crying in emotional outbursts were hardly a preparation for comforting a widow coming to terms with her husband's death and deceit!

"Now your question," she continued. "Was his love for them false? No, of course not. It was me he didn't love and probably never had. And, if you were to ask, despite all he did, yes, I did once love him. If I had been able to accept that he had affairs – some women do accept that I know - then we would not have become such silent enemies.

"Did your daughters understand that it was you he didn't love, not them?"

"Oh yes. I don't need to tell you surely that children pick up a great deal and they have watched his indifference to me over many years."

"Well…"

"You are right of course. Are you telling me that I don't have to tell them all I know?"

"I really don't know," he replied.

"So you think I should let them go on loving him regardless of how he behaved to me and other people?"

"Marjorie, I really don't know but I think I've learnt that children have a way of only taking in what they are ready to understand. In time, when they ask, you might find that you can tell them what they want to know."

"But keeping these terrible secrets…."

"I guess that would be hard…"

"But you think I should do it?"

Brian seemed to have given her advice without actually meaning to do so! Perhaps he had given her what she wanted – appreciation for her predicament. Perhaps that was all anyone could do for her. Now, he wanted to escape. He was afraid of her developing a dependence on him or even worse, that she wanted affection from him. He was in a vulnerable state himself, fearing deep down that he was in the process of losing Polly.

He replied cautiously. "That seems to be the conclusion you have reached for the moment. Which of us knows how things in life will develop."

"Perhaps you are right." She smiled at him and he took this as an opportunity to rise as if to go.

"Is there anything else I can do?"

"You have been most kind."

She was back in control. He had glimpsed her private world. He was as perplexed as she was.

At the door, she said: "Do you want to take your wife's painting with you? I really have nowhere to hang it and I don't want to keep anything that came from his life outside the life we shared here in the family. It was in the flat, over the bed."

She fetched the painting and he left with it under his arm. As he placed it carefully in the boot of his car, he repeated to himself the phrase 'over the bed'. Marjorie had indeed told him before that she found Polly's painting in the London flat but not that it had hung *over the bed.* For the first time, an unwelcome thought assailed him. Polly's painting was over the bed because Polly and Tom had slept together in that bed! He recalled that the VC had joked bitterly that Tom's London flat might have been purchased "to house his mistress." Now the shocking possibility was, could this have been Polly?

He started the car and drove out of the drive, conscious of Marjorie waiting at the window to wave good bye, but so shaken was he that he stopped a little further down the empty, private road, out of her sight, and switched off the engine to think. His hands went to cover his face. Over what must be about a year and a half, he had occasionally feared that Polly might have looked for a lover but he had always brushed such a thought from his mind. He had wondered about the many term-time evenings when she had been so often late home, but he had understood the demands of her job and of her commitment to its success and had assured himself of her total work obsession. Her gradual emotional distancing from him he explained as a product of his own depression and the fact that it irritated and nonplussed her. Polly tackled problems head-on and she would have been frustrated that she could not tackle his problem head-on because it was *his* problem. When she had driven off to Cumbria, which seemed illogical, he had fleetingly wondered whether someone else was seeing her in this out-of-the-way place but had dismissed that as fantasy; whoever would be prepared to spend three months in such a spot in the midst of a raging epidemic of foot and mouth disease? But – and the thought had an instant logic to it – what if the lover had been dead? Supposing she had been one of Tom's many women, the most recent perhaps, she might conceivably have escaped there to recover from the shock of his death and, yes, from the possibility of the discovery of the affair. Why had he not thought of this before? It tied up.

As he re-started the car and drove back into the city, he was scarcely aware of the delays in the traffic or of the rain that beat on the windscreen, making the wipers squeak and thump with tedious regularity. With such regularity, he had allowed time to move tediously onward and thus he had missed the now startlingly obvious possibility that Polly and Tom had been having an affair – begun most probably with the purchase of the very painting now sitting in the back of his car. No wonder Marjorie didn't want to give it house-room! Did she know? Is that why she told him so much about Tom, leaving him to form his own conclusions? Would he ask her? And then again - would he ask Polly?

Term had ended for Easter and over the next few days, before Polly's scheduled return, he went about his life in a bad dream. His imagination devised scenes of Tom and Polly in bed together. He raged at Tom for what he now thought of as his callous disregard for Marjorie, his wife, for himself, Brian, and, ultimately for Polly, as he was clearly the kind of man to start an affair and as easily terminate it. All the kind things Tom had said to him about his, Brian's, work, were all flattery to cover up the fact that he was having it off with his wife. He had even defended the man when the VC began to cast doubts on his integrity. Who was the fool here? Not the VC. Not Tom. He was! He, Brian, the fall-guy. The cuckold! And Polly? What was Polly thinking all this time? Was she also making a fool of him? And now. When he told her all the stuff about Tom, she said nothing.

A long few days followed. He did not go into the College. He sat doing nothing at his desk during the day and moved about the house at night-time, in and out of rooms. He slept late into the mornings and then fell asleep early over the TV in the evenings in his chair. He would then haul himself into a bed that was never made from one night to the next. He didn't shave. He didn't shop. He didn't cook but ate up the bits of bread and greying ham and dry cheese in the fridge. He didn't call Miles or Jessica. He left the answer-phone on in case they or the College – or worse, Marjorie Frost – should call. By the end of the week, he was exhausted.

*   *   *

The time came for Veronica's final sitting. Alice saw her again driving into Polly's yard and followed her in to greet her as she opened her car door.

"Is everything all right with the painter lady?" she asked. "I've seen you there a few times and not seen her about at all for a day or two and wondered if she were took ill with 'flu' or something."

"No, she's fine." Veronica answered cheerily.

"Well, I just wondered." Alice showed no sign of letting Veronica get out of the car. "She must get a bit lonely now that her daughter's gone back and she's bashed her car up a bit I see," pointing at long scratches on the wing.

"I think she's busy painting before she goes back to London."

"Still finding things to paint then even if she can't be getting about?"

"Oh I think so."

"And you like what she paints?"

"It's very interesting, yes."

Alice was still blocking her exit from the car. "Is it then?" she said non-committally. "I wouldn't know about that of course, but if you say so. Jonty thinks so too, I dare say."

＊　　　　　　＊　　　　　　＊

"Who were you talking to? Polly asked her as she opened the door.

"Just Alice."

"Is she checking up on me?"

"I guess she was."

Polly had pulled the easel from its corner, replaced the incomplete painting of the pyre with the portrait and was ready to conduct the sitting. Veronica thought she had become very professional, wanting to distance herself from the distress of their last meeting. For her part, Polly was intent on capturing the astonishing strength of Veronica's character. She had now learnt never to equate social attitudes with a person's age. If being eighty was relevant at all, it was that she had lived through a period of dramatic social change and personal disappointment and had become strong as a result. She began to study her sitter again. It was easier to search for her character in a portrait than to try to explain her.

After a quarter of an hour, Polly paused. "You said I was strong and would get through this."

"I did say that and I do believe that."

"I've had another telephone call from Brian."

"And are there more rumours?"

"Oh yes. This story is going to run. Tom was fraudulently financing his private enterprises with research money"

"Really. How extraordinary."

Veronica had set off for Milnethwaite not knowing quite what else she could do or say to assist her friend but determined that this woman whom she admired should not allow herself to be weakened or destroyed. Polly for her part had been trying to imagine how she could possibly return to London while the investigations into Tom's financial affairs were in progress as well as the fact that Jessica knew of her affair. How long could her involvement stay hidden.

Veronica, as if reading her thoughts, asked, "You said that no-one else knew about your affair?"

" That was before my daughter's visit. I told her after she had found a portrait of Tom beside my bed."

Veronica sighed. There were rarely neat and easy solutions to problems.

"When I told her," Polly explained, " I believed that the excuse for my behaviour, of which she totally disapproved of course, lay in the authenticity of my love for Tom and that I could no longer tell lies about it and that, above all, I couldn't lie to my daughter, for her sake as well as for my own. But now? That wasn't true, as it has turned out."

"And what has she done about what you told her, which was true in your case at the time wasn't it?"

"Nothing yet. She phoned yesterday to urge me not to tell him of the affair in case it led to our marriage breaking down – which she dreads. "

"Of course she does."

"And my son rang to say that the young woman he loved but who had a husband and child already, had finished with him and returned to her husband. As he finished the call, he said that I had been lucky in marrying his father."

"And you said to him?"

"I dodged."

"So they are putting you under pressure to go back to them and your husband." Polly nodded.

"And your husband?"

"He's afraid I came here to get away from him."

"Whereas?"

" I came here to get over Tom and thought I couldn't face Brian until I had."

Both women were silent. It was Veronica who spoke.

"Can we go back over what we said yesterday ? If Tom were alive, what would you do?"

"I'd be angry with the Vice Chancellor for accusing Tom of malpractice without the evidence yet clear and …… I'd ask Tom to tell me the truth."

"What difference does it make that he's dead?"

"I don't understand." This thought startled Polly. " I can't ask him……" her words petered out in uncertainty.

"What would you ask him if he were alive?"

"Did you use funds fraudulently?"

"Anything else?"

"Do you love me?"

"And what would he say to that?"

"He would say he did."

"Would you believe him?"

Polly stopped her work and spoke slowly and deliberately. "No. This has been a time of truth for me and I don't much like it."

"Feeling like that, what would you have done about him."

"I hope I would have finished it."

Then, as if it were a non-sequitur, Polly's next words did not altogether surprise Veronica.

"Brian said the Vice Chancellor asked him if Tom had crashed the car on purpose intending to kill himself."

"I had wondered about that. Could he have done?"

Polly sighed. " I might almost wish that it was true and that there could have been a note to me saying that he could no longer keep up the deceptions on which his life was built! But I was at the inquest. He swung off the road to avoid a lorry. I couldn't tell Brian that without confessing that I had attended the Inquest."

There was another long pause while Polly resumed painting. Then she stopped again.

"I am painting two pictures at the same time; your portrait and the pyre. And I have been trying to unravel a connection between them in my mind."

"How do you mean?"

"It might be easier to paint than explain. I don't yet know, but it is as if this epidemic, dreadful in its own right, is a sort of metaphor - for our times, if you like"

"I'm listening."

"The virus is out of control here isn't it? Ethel describes its spread and mismanagement as stemming from the way farming had changed to accommodate to our urban demand for cheap food. A disaster waiting to happen."

"I'm with you so far"

"Tom didn't kill himself, but *he* was out of control. He was playing his life too fast, as if he had succumbed to a sort of 21st century urban virus, when you think you can have and do anything and everything and get away with it, by deception if necessary."

"And you?"

"I succumbed to it too but for my quite separate reasons. It was a 'folie-a-deux, except that the two of us were part of something bigger – a 'folie-a-mille' if there were to be such a thing. I was snatching an escape from my doubt that I had the originality to be a painter. I vaguely knew that I was neglecting Brian and my children, but told myself they were too grown-up to need me any more."

Veronica nodded in understanding.

"The 'siege-time' that I thought was for grieving, has turned into a time to rid myself of self-delusion."

"I think I see." Veronica said.

Polly nodded and resumed painting. Then she stopped.

"I am shocked not so much now that Tom betrayed me and others including his wife, but that I betrayed Brian. You understood how I got into the affair because you knew how you came to sleep with your husband secretly, but you didn't betray anyone did you? His wife, for instance?"

"That was a great worry to us both, but, you see, she had dementia. I am still not sure that that was a sufficient excuse."

"I see, at least I think I do."

"Well, he, we, had no opportunity to put it right.'

"And I do, you mean."

There was a long silence while Polly painted.

"They will come to know the truth" said Polly at last, "but I don't yet know how or when. It may be impossible, it may even be wrong, but I want to re-establish myself with them first and then see how best to do it. I want to be able to say how wrong I was, without excuses."

Veronica smiled one of the smiles that Polly loved. It was not one of approval or disapproval. It was simply one of understanding. "How does the portrait of me come into the equation? You said the paintings had something in common."

"These conversations. Your honesty and your wisdom if that doesn't sound too pompous." Veronica waved her hand to downplay such a verdict but Polly laughed and added "and your steadfastness! You're like Ethel in that respect. Good Cumbrian women! I would hope to get through all this and become a bit more like you both."

Veronica said that she suddenly felt extremely tired. She had not had such demand made on her mental capacities for years. She smiled again at Polly.

"Do you think we need a drink?"
Polly duly got up to pour them each a whisky before returning to her easel.

"To you for pulling me through this," she said, raising her glass.

"Thank you for paying me the compliment of painting my portrait."

Polly turned again to the canvas and after a little more work, looked up directly at Veronica.

"May I ask you? Did *you* lie to keep your affair with your husband quiet?"

"It was a secret, yes, but I had no need to lie," was Veronica's reply, adding, with a smile, "but Robert did. He lied. He lied to protect his wife, not himself or me."

'Ah." Polly stood away from the portrait to see if it was finished. The slight changes she had made to the mouth and eyes had the desired effect of bringing Veronica alive. She seemed at last to have caught the enigma of her character.

"Come and see the portrait," she said.

After Veronica had left, Polly pondered her friend's last words. They had made her ashamed. She had thought only of protecting herself. She busied herself with putting away the canvas and sorting out her painting materials and, because she was suddenly very tired, went early to bed. But she didn't sleep. She lay awake but in an entirely new state of mind. For nearly two years, she had been preoccupied with her own injured psychological state. At last she became aware of an overwhelming compassion and love for Brian. What she had done had been wrong and wronging. She sighed his name and wept. Any tears were now for him.

Chapter Ten

On March 30th, the largest number of cases was reported in one day and on April 1st, 622,000 animals were awaiting disposal in Cumbria. From then on until September 2001, when the disease was eradicated, the number of outbreaks diminished.

The inquest into Eric Stewart's death was carried out more quickly than expected. The verdict was never in doubt. The local paper carried the story on its front page the same evening.

"Local Farmer Shoots Himself in Grief"

The Inquest was held today on the death of Eric Stewart, 73, a farmer from Firsgate, near Longtown, who died on March 22nd. The coroner pronounced a verdict of death by suicide. Mr Stewart, well-known in the Longtown Auction, took his own life two weeks after his prize herd of 400 Friesians was slaughtered on March 8th. The court was told that Mr Stewart had been building up his family herd for over thirty years. "He saw it as part of his family," Annie his widow told our special reporter. "After they'd been shot, he could not bear to see them in the fields waiting so long for burial." The coroner warned the government that the long delays between culling and the disposal of carcasses were causing unnecessary distress to local farmers.

Eric Stewart is one of hundreds of farmers caught in the throes of this epidemic that is so far ten times greater than any previous one. Today 50 new cases were reported in the country. If the movements of beasts had been halted as soon as the first pig was diagnosed positive on 20th February, then Mr Stewart would still be alive. "The epidemic has been a catalogue of incompetence from start to finish' according to Mr Stewart's brother, Jim Stewart, 75, who farms in Milnethwaite in West Cumbria and whose herd has so far escaped the disease. "The government ought to have my brother's death upon their conscience for letting it spread so far and so fast," he said.

The funeral will be held on Monday, April 2nd at St. Hilda's Church, Firstown, at 12 noon. Only close relatives are allowed to attend, due to restrictions still in force in the area. No flowers but any donations to the Cumbrian Farm Crisis Network.'

Sunday, April 1st.

Polly awoke early to a bright Sunday morning. She sat up at once wide-awake. She had less than a fortnight before her sabbatical came to an end. She turned on the local radio to hear the day's tally of the huge piles of animals awaiting disposal. She dressed quickly and walked up to the church from where she could see the fells emerging from mist and could catch the remaining pink of the dawn behind the farm-house. She went into the church, well before the usual 8 o'clock service. She liked to sit there. The church was small, with a wonderful arch at the chancel steps, which gave the white interior an atmosphere that, for someone like herself with no religious belief whatsoever, would find immensely calming. This morning she sat reading a local church newspaper, which she had picked up from the table on her way in. It was about the epidemic and quoted the experience of families caught up in it. She read:

> *"We have been said to have poisoned and destroyed the wildlife and the countryside. We are accused of being cruel to animals, spreading disease to the public, of being unreasonable to walkers, and now wickedly destroying the tourist industry…..and such criticism takes its toll….We have worked from dawn to dusk and beyond, year in and year out for the last thirty years…. As I write we are waiting to see whether the Government…is going ahead to kill half of our healthy flocks of sheep that are on the Cumbrian farms for winter."*

The writer concluded that it was illogical to preserve the barns and walls but destroy the community that created them.

She had put aside the painting of the pyre, not wanting to finish it until she knew how to do so. So many things had happened since that morning. Now, she felt ready at last to resume what she saw as her major work – not the depiction of Mellbreak, although now that quite pleased her, but the pyre, the biggest challenge yet to her craft.

As she came out of the church porch and turned for home, she caught sight of Jonty coming down the lane after milking. She had not seen him since their ill-fated encounter. She now saw that event too in a different light. Jonty's behaviour that day epitomised the tensions of his life. Instead of turning away from him as she would have done before today, she stood and waited for him to come closer. She smiled to herself to think that it was too early for Alice to see them. She had worked out Alice's role in the village as a watchman calling the hours and a bit more besides. Jonty saw her waiting and hesitated whether to turn away. When she waved, he walked slowly towards her.

"Hello, Jonty. I want to thank you for your note. I appreciated your apology, " Polly said. "I'm glad you wrote it and I shall say nothing to anyone about what happened. So we can consider it to belong in the past, can we?"

Jonty, deeply embarrassed, removed his cap, a gesture reminiscent of their first meeting. "Thank you very much, Mrs Creed."

"Please call me Polly. How are your parents since your family tragedy?"

"Kind of you to ask. They are as well as to be expected." He grinned at the cliché and Polly smiled too. "My Dad is better now they've got the army in and my mother is getting over it as she always does."

"She's a fine woman," Polly said. "I shall miss her. My last day here will be Good Friday."

"She'll miss you too. You've been very kind to her."

"And she to me. It has been a dreadful time for you all."

"Not over yet, but thank you." He wanted to say that he would miss her too and that Good Friday would seem like Black Friday to him, but he dared not say the words forming in his head. Instead he said, "my father has had such a shock, that I think he'll gradually pass things over to me."

"Is that okay by you? Your mum told me you'd never really wanted to farm."

"Do we ever get all we want," Jonty said, "but it now seems the right thing to happen. We'll all make changes to avoid such things happening again."

She began to move away when a thought struck her and she turned back. "Would you like to see my last painting before I go – the one of the pyre. I should finish it early next week to give it time to dry before I take it away with me."

He was further embarrassed as this was the sketch that had sent him off the rails and caused him to say those dreadful things to her.

"Would you really let me?"

"I should like your opinion very much."

He blurted out, "If you are sure you can trust me?"

"I am sure I can. What about Wednesday of next week, my last week. I shall have to pack up after that as I plan to leave on the Saturday. "

He coloured with pleasure and put back his cap and watched her as she walked off to the barn. Last night he had noticed her light on late again. He would miss knowing she was there even though he no longer allowed himself quite so many fantasies about her.

So, on the bright morning of April 1st, All Fools Day, and, according to the church notice-board 'Passion Sunday', she walked back to the barn, uncovered the painting of the pyre and began to work. She worked on it with total concentration day after day, sleeping well at nights and rising early to carry on each morning, walking down the lane to clear her head and hand from time to time. She did not remove Tom from the foreground but painted over him so that he was invisible to all but her.

From that Sunday the number of outbreaks began to dwindle until the footpaths were opened once again in June.

*   *   *

Brian woke on Sunday morning, suddenly clear what he would do. He was aware that a change had taken place. What changed him was remembering, as he woke, that when he had asked Polly, in his state of unknowing and unsuspecting, whether she was coming home, he had said that he worried that her sabbatical was a chance to get away from him. She had replied, "Not from you, Brian. Perhaps from myself." She wouldn't say that had she not meant it. She had never been so self-reflective in recent years.

Was it possible that she had changed too? His spirits lifted. After all, if she had been in love with Tom Frost, which was after all only speculation on his part, he was now dead!

The answer to the question that had been whirling around in his head for days was suddenly clear. What was he going to do? He would do nothing. Nothing, in this situation was something. Action. A positive action of self-discipline. It was cryptic. He had not asked her what she meant and she had not elaborated. If he had no proof that Polly had an affair with Tom and he could therefore have been making it all up, then why not leave things as they were? Unspoken. Like a landscape that they would know but not need to describe, that they could walk across without questioning.

He pulled the bedding off the bed to wash it and then began to tidy the house. He stopped once in the middle of hoovering the living room carpet and sat down in his favourite chair and briefly wept. He could not remember weeping since his childhood. He was now sure of the rightness of his plan. He would not risk losing her by accusing her of anything. If what he feared were true, then it would be up to her to tell him if she chose to do so. Even if it were true, it was at an end. One day in the future they might talk about Tom - Tom the charismatic success who had charmed him, deceived women and misused them all. He might come to feel sorry for him. That Tom was dead and was now the loser, did not make Brian the winner, but he was alive and loved his wife.

*   *   *

On Monday, April 2nd, Jim and Ethel and Jonty travelled over to Firstown for the funeral. They went straight to the village church. They could not enter the farm. Annie met them at the church gate. There were very few people there; her daughter and family were briefly allowed to leave the contaminated farm, and so they stood in the cold morning air beside the bio-security barrier, watching as the funeral car drove slowly down the village street. It was unlike a normal village funeral, when the whole village would have walked silently behind the coffin from their houses to the church. Now people were standing at their windows watching as the car passed by. The police and the press were in attendance, the press with their cameras focused on the slow-moving coffin.

Annie, supported by Jim, walked without tears down the church path behind the coffin. Ethel followed, arm in arm with Jonty. The service was short. MAFF and NFU officials and one or two local people, none of them from the local farms who were barred from leaving their land, came in quietly and sat at the back, the men in their dark, funeral suits. The police prevented the press from entering. At the front of the church was an island of intimacy; isolated by the siege, the two brothers were now together, with their wives close by them. Jonty thought of them as standing, at that moment, for the whole scandal of the epidemic and its cruel assault on the farming community.

Eric was buried in the church graveyard, daffodils coming into flower around the spot.

"Buried like his cows," Annie said.

Annie had received hundreds of letters from people all around the district and from people wider afield who had read of Eric's death in the national papers.

"It won't bring him back," Annie said to Ethel. "He just didn't want to start all over again. I'll move into a bungalow after all this is over. We had it planned already for the future."

Jonty drove Jim and Ethel back to Milnethwaite in silence.

As they drove into the village, Jim said " We might not get it, lass. It's dying down."

"By the grace of God," said Ethel.

He replied, "I'm sorry to both of you for my temper!"

"You old fool!" said Ethel, touching his knee.

*   *   *

Jonty called in during the week to see the finished painting and stayed about a quarter of an hour gazing at it, speechless.

"It shows," he said, "the top and bottom of the tragedy."

"Loss and fire and waste and bloody mistakes!" Polly said. Jonty suggested that, on Good Friday, he would like to carry it on its easel into the churchyard by the lych-gate for people to look at as they passed by.

*   *   *

Good Friday

And so, all through Good Friday, Polly's last full day, when the daffodils were blowing plentifully in the wind and sunshine, the painting stood on its easel by the lych-gate for people to stop and wonder at. Alice, Ethel and the vicar took turns to be on duty to protect it and the press came to photograph it. Jonty himself was interviewed beside it for BBC regional television but Polly, busy packing, chose to stay out of sight after one quick photograph of her beside it.

During Saturday morning, Veronica called to say good bye and to tell Polly that she was to move back to Carlisle the following week. From there, she would sell Robert's house when the epidemic was finally over. They vowed to keep in touch and she promised to come and see the portrait if it were ever on show. They parted with great affection. Polly wanted her to have the portrait but she refused.

"Who have I to leave it to?" she said.

Polly rang Ethel to say a long and fond goodbye, promising to return once the epidemic was over and urgently hoping that they continued to avoid it. She promised to leave her final cheque as she drove away. In the event she would also give her a framed drawing of the barn and leave it beside the farm gate.

Polly then telephoned Miles to say she would come and see him very soon. She then rang Jessica to confirm the time of her return and to assure her that it was not her responsibility to keep her parents together because she, Polly, would do everything in her power to avoid a break-up.

"Will you improve on the truth?"

"We shall see." Polly smiled.

"I am glad you'll be at home again," said Jessica.

"Me too," said Polly near to tears.

Finally, she rang Brian to confirm the time of her return.

"I'll get us a good Sunday lunch," he said "like the old times"

She drove off the next day with a pegged rug, some old frames, a pile of drawing boards and three large canvases carefully wrapped in the back of the car.

The End

Acknowledgments

1. "Lessons Learned" Report of Professor Roy Anderson into the 2001 FMD outbreak in England and Wales (2002)

2. "The 2001 Outbreak of Foot and Mouth Disease": National Audit Office Report by the Comptroller and Auditor General HC939 June 2002) Extract: "*At least 57 farms had already been infected with the virus when the disease was confirmed on 20 February 2001, The disease spread quickly and there were outbreaks in 44 counties, unitary authorities and metropolitan districts and over 2000 premises were infected. The scale and impact of the epidemic were immense: greater than that of the last serious outbreak in Britain in 1967-68. In mid-April 2001 at the height of the crisis more than 10,000 vets, soldiers, field and support staff, assisted by thousands more working for contractors were engaged in fighting the disease. Up to 100,000 animals were slaughtered and disposed of each day in what was a massive and complex logistical operation. Tourism suffered the largest financial impact from the outbreak with visitors to Britain and the countryside deterred by the closure of footpaths by local authorities and media images of mass pyres.*"

3. "The Health and Social Consequences of the 2001 Foot and Mouth Disease Epidemic in North Cumbria" (2004) by Dr Maggie Mort, Dr Ian Covey,Dr Cathy Bailey and Josephine Baxter from the Institute for Health Research, University of Lancaster.

4. The Anguish of the Killing Fields: Special report: "Three farming families relate their experiences and fears": by Hilary Wilson in the Way (April 2001) the Newspaper of the Diocese of Carlisle, quoted in the Epilogue.

5. Cumbrian Farm Crisis Network: Brian Armstrong, who lost his animals in the epidemic, for advice. Susan Wilkinson, Somerset Farm Crisis Network who checked for farm accuracy

6. "You cannot improve on the truth" is a quotation from "Venture into the Interior" by Laurence van der Post

7. Rose Gaete (The Literary Consultancy), Frank my husband, Gillian Manns, Janice Collins, Janet Ansell, Averil Slade, Alma Cullen, Sue Keen and a few other friends who read the story.

8. Many friends from West Cumbria

9. Teresa Benison, Cambridge University Continuing Education Creative Writing Course 2002.

Acronyms

FMD – Foot and Mouth Disease

MAFF – Ministry of Agriculture, Fisheries and Food subsumed into DEFRA- Department of Environment, Food and Rural Affairs .

NADFAS –The NationalAssociation of Decorative and Fine Arts Societies.

NFU – National Farmers Union

UCCA now called UCAS – Universities and Colleges Admissions Service